TH

Conceived in darkest chao
age—until nothing could
its desire for destruction

THE CHILD

Julian was only an innocent babe—or so he seemed. Hidden within him dwelled a power that none could fathom or dare to challenge.

ANIMUS

As old as time, as wicked as sin, the child came with a deadly grin....

A SPELLBINDING TALE OF RELENTLESS TERROR BY ED KELLEHER & HARRIETTE VIDAL

ANIMUS

ED KELLEHER & HARRIETTE VIDAL

LEISURE BOOKS NEW YORK CITY

A LEISURE BOOK®

July 1993

Published by

Dorchester Publishing Co., Inc.
276 Fifth Avenue
New York, NY 10001

"Between astonishment and grief, I was tearless."
—Lord Byron

ANIMUS

Prologue

Nantucket Island, 1967.

The room was impossibly pink. Designed by a decorator who had been deprived as a child, it was little-girl perfect. The space was lined with pink and white shelves holding scores of antique dolls from around the world. The dolls' sightless eyes stared out at the opulence in the room. There were games of every dimension. Some, much too sophisticated for an eight year old. Hundreds of books, ranging from pop-up antique volumes to preteen encyclopedias, stood immaculately on polished shelves. A handmade wooden dollhouse dominated one corner of the room. The house and the furnishings inside were exact replicas of the main house in which the little girl lived. In the diminutive rooms, a family of dolls lived in sterile splendor. The dollhouse alone cost $10,000.

But it was the pink that made one gasp upon first entering the room. It was everywhere. It was a decorator's fantasy of what little girls are made of. The shades of pink—incarnadine, flesh, coral—practically exploded like puffy cotton candy. They shaded the walls, the curtains and shutters, the pillows and the frilly canopy on top of the four-poster bed.

The overall effect of the room was breathtaking. But one couldn't help noticing that the chamber was almost too tidy for a living child to play and sleep there. No crayon-drawn pictures decorated any of the walls. No stuffed animal lay on the floor as if dropped there when something else caught the child's attention. The very precise order of the room made for an uncomfortable feeling. The fingers of sun poking through the shutters seemed to highlight in precision the beautiful, dark-haired child sitting at the round table in the center of the room.

Catherine Bellamy's slim body seemed almost tense as she hunched over a large piece of construction paper. Her fingers grasped a black crayon as she drew a picture on the paper. In fact, she was tense, nervous. The picture was to be a present for her father. It had to be perfect—just like her daddy expected Catherine to be.

Animus

Catherine's wide hazel eyes studied the drawing. She placed the black crayon back in the box. She needed another color for her father's suit. That was how she worked—never leaving the crayon she had just finished using on the table for later. That wasn't orderly. She always returned them to the box before she took another color. Her daddy demanded that she be neat, orderly. And she had to be perfect for her father. She couldn't disappoint him.

Catherine frowned. She brushed strands of chestnut-colored hair back from her forehead. Her face was a sweet, childish oval, accentuated by long eyelashes and a pert, freckled nose. Her mouth was heart shaped and, for the moment, a little severe as she pondered an eight year old's dilemma.

It seemed as if, no matter how hard she tried, she was always disappointing her daddy. She wished she had a mother. Maybe another girl would understand her better. Daddies were men. They were busy with other things, especially her daddy. He was so busy he hardly even noticed Catherine—except for the times when she disappointed him. Then he got mad.

The young girl shook her head. She shouldn't think like that. She had to concentrate on her picture. She looked in the crayon box. There was a space where the blue crayon should have been. Catherine shook her head knowingly.

"Okay, Bobo," she said. "Where did you put the blue? You know I need it for Daddy's suit."

Catherine looked quickly around the room. "Bobo?"

She cocked her head to one side. From off in the distance, she could hear the faint hum of the pump in the aquarium. She looked out the window for a moment, distracted, forgetting her coloring for the moment. The full oak tree blocked her view of the woods beyond. Catherine loved to sit in the crook of that tree. She could reach it with hardly any trouble if she leaned out just a bit from her window seat. She had to wait until no one was around to sit there. Little ladies didn't sit in trees.

A faint movement out of the corner of her eye made Catherine remember the task at hand. She looked down at her drawing.

"Bobo? Where's the blue crayon?" She paused. "Bobo, I asked you a question."

A shadow brushed Catherine's face. "You put it back in the box?" Catherine looked in the Crayola box, then nodded. "Oh, here it is."

The little girl ran her hands down the ruffled sundress as if to iron out any wrinkles before she started coloring in her drawing with long, heavy strokes. "There's his blue suit," she murmured, satisfied with her work. "Daddy's going to love this, Bobo."

Catherine stiffened. Her voice rose. "He will not hate it! You be quiet. He will love it and he will buy me a new doll and he'll take me on a picnic and we'll go out in a boat and he'll tell me I'm his princess and . . . and you be quiet!"

Animus

With one more wide stroke of the crayon, Catherine finished the picture. She held it up to the light, examining every detail. She nodded. Still holding the drawing, Catherine got up and walked to her bedroom door. She looked back at the empty, pink room.

"I know he'll love this, Bobo."

But she didn't sound convinced. Not even in her own mind.

Catherine entered her father's bedroom on tiptoes. The room frightened her. The dark mahogany furniture loomed upward, casting shadows in unlikely places. The huge king-size bed with perfectly ironed silk sheets didn't seem as if it was made for sleeping. Not to a little girl. There wasn't a speck of dust to be seen.

The room was empty, but Catherine heard running water coming from the adjacent bathroom. A spiky line of brightness came from the partly open door.

Catherine walked through the bedroom. She grasped her drawing in her small hands.

"Daddy?"

No reply.

Catherine reached the bathroom. She pushed the door open wider. Her father, clad in an elegant powder-blue bathrobe, was preparing to shave. His shaving paraphernalia was lined up neatly on the marble sink.

Catherine wrinkled her eyes. She studied her father's image in the mirror for a moment. He was very handsome. She had heard the grown-ups say so.

Jason Bellamy noticed his little girl. He frowned slightly. "Catherine."

He saw the way she jumped when he spoke. It annoyed him. He didn't know why he scared his daughter. After all, he had never struck the child, and he gave her everything she wanted. Jason sighed.

"Catherine, can't you see I'm busy?"

The little girl was too excited to be dismissed. With pride, she offered her father the sketch.

"I have a present for you, Daddy," Catherine said timidly.

Still annoyed, Jason Bellamy took the drawing roughly from his daughter's outstretched hand. Then his frown softened. Catherine had labored over the crude sketch of him. She so wanted his approval.

If only Catherine hadn't chosen that moment to speak . . . .

"Bobo said you wouldn't like this, Daddy. But I know you will."

"Catherine, I've warned you before about this Bobo nonsense." Jason Bellamy crumpled the sketch in his hand. "You're a little too old now to be talking to imaginary playmates. Do you hear me?" he asked through clenched teeth.

Catherine's lip trembled. Her spirit broken, she whispered, "Yes."

Seeing the small figure of his daughter—his flesh and blood—back down so quickly only made Jason want to hurt her more. "Bobo is not real. You made him up. If I hear his name again, you'll be sorry. And don't start with the tears. I'm in no mood for that."

Gulping air to keep the tears back, Catherine looked at her father pleadingly. "Bobo's my friend. My real friend. He listens to me. He cares about me. I didn't make him up."

Jason Bellamy thrust the crumpled drawing at Catherine. His voice got louder and angrier. "You did make him up. And if you know what's good for you, you'll stop acting like a baby."

Head down, Catherine took the rejected drawing from her father. "Bobo's real."

Jason exploded. "That's enough, young lady! I want you to go to your room. I'll deal with you later. Do you hear me?"

Hurt and dejected, Catherine turned, still clutching her ruined sketch. She left her father alone. She walked like someone with a heavy burden upon her shoulders. But not for a moment did she cry.

Catherine trudged down the hallway toward her bedroom. Once in the haven of her pink chamber, she threw herself on the quilt-covered bed.

"He's mean, Bobo," she murmured. "He doesn't love me. You're the only one who loves me. I hate him. I wish somebody would teach him a lesson. I wish someone would hurt him. I wish he would love me, Bobo."

Meanwhile, Jason Bellamy stared at his face in the bathroom mirror. How could a little girl make him this uneasy? His own daughter! He shook his head as if to clear all thoughts from his mind.

Jason began spreading the thick, creamy lather on his face. He did it with slow, even strokes, barely paying attention to the action. He dipped the razor into the steamy water and began shaving his face—taking off the lather and whiskers, dunking the razor back into the hot water, repeating those actions until one entire side of his face was clean.

The steam from the water began to create a mist on the bathroom mirror. Jason wiped off the condensation with a towel and began shaving the other side of his face. But something was wrong. Although his hands had become unsteady, Jason paid no attention to the trembling in his fingers. Slowly, he raked the razor across his face. He never saw the thin piece of skin, the blood mixed with the shaving cream, as he sliced into the other side of his face. He barely felt the jab of pain as he dug the razor in deeper with each movement of the blade. The water in the sink turned crimson, the bubbles from the lather making the mixture appear almost pretty. It wasn't until the gash in his face was so deep it nearly went into the bone that he realized what was happening. By then, it was too late. The damage to his handsome face was done. Jason Bellamy stared at the open flap of skin on his cheek. The physical pain wasn't as horrifying as the act itself. What had come over him? He had no recollection of cutting himself. As the blood made a lazy trail down his face onto his chin, stopping there for a moment and then dripping onto the sink, he thought he saw something out of the corner of his eye. No. Not something. Someone. A small, dark-haired boy. It was only for a fleeting moment. Then nothing. As if coming out of a deep trance, Jason moved quickly to grab a towel from the rack. He pressed it against his torn face.

Catherine Bellamy screamed just as her father was turning to leave the bathroom to call for help.

Jason collided with his daughter, who was standing by the bathroom door. Still holding her drawing in her hands, the little girl was screaming hysterically. She had seen everything. Bobo had told her he was going to hurt her father. She hadn't believed him. Bobo was always saying things like that when her father was mean. But never before had he actually carried out any of his threats.

She had run back to the bathroom just to make sure Bobo was not going to do anything. There was something about the way he said her father was going to pay for hurting her. Something in his voice that only she could hear in her head. Something nasty and final. How had Bobo made her daddy do this to himself?

When the ambulance arrived, just a few minutes later, it wasn't just Jason Bellamy who rode in the back of the vehicle. Heavily sedated, Catherine lay on the stretcher while her father, face wrapped in bandages, looked at her. It was a hell of a thing for a child to witness. No wonder she was hysterical. For a split second, Jason Bellamy reached out and smoothed his daughter's hair, moving it away from her pale, damp face. The tenderness didn't last long. At that moment, Catherine's eyes flew wide. She stared directly at her father. Never before had Jason seen such pure hatred. It didn't even look like his daughter lying there. For the first time in his life, Jason knew the meaning of terror. Not even what he just did to his face was as frightening as looking down at his daughter. Jason drew his hand back. The little girl smiled before she lost consciousness.

There is no time. There are no senses. There is darkness. And then the floating.

It is not like sleep. Or at least any sleep that Catherine ever had before.

There are no dreams. There is no hope to get up.

And this nonfeeling grows within her, filling her entire body.

Since there is no sense of time, she doesn't know how long this has been happening. But at some point, she becomes aware. Of small things at first—then before.

But even this awareness cannot help her communicate.

She is without movement. She is without eyesight. She can hear but it is at a distance. Sounds are muffled. She is not aware of where she is. But she is aware of an ache. An ache within her body. Slowly, at first, it builds, till it is a blinding pain. She cannot cry out. She can only wonder. Where is she? What is happening to her?

And then slowly memory returns. She knows who she is. She remembers the past. Her baby. What happened to her baby? She cannot run her hands down her body to see.

At some point, she realizes she is in a hospital. She can hear. She can hear people sobbing. She can hear Ian's angry voice. How dare he be angry with her. And what is wrong with these people? Why are they crying?

She's fine. She's alive.

She doesn't know when she realized she was in a coma. Her eyes did not even move behind her lids. She wondered if she was on life support. After more time goes by, she realizes she isn't. She's a vegetable. Just lying there. And her baby is gone. Is he alive? She'll have to listen to the conversations as they take place around her, try to catch words about her baby.

Fingers of loneliness touch her secret parts, touch all her senses, as they slowly return. Still, she cannot move. She cannot show the people around her she can understand and hear them.

There is no sense of wakefulness. No sense of sleep. There is just a sense of being.

At some point, she hears a child crying. Where is the sound coming from? Is it her imagination? Can one have an imagination in a coma?

Someone is pricking her feet with a pin. There is no pain, but the sensation of feeling is there. Perhaps she'll be able to open her eyes soon. Perhaps she'll hear the child crying again. There is a sense that tells her it's crying out for her. It is a boy. She knows instinctively it is her baby.

Cool and slippery, a voice steals into her mind. It tells her everything is going to be okay. It tells her not to worry. It tells her it will seek revenge. But it does not reassure her that she will wake up from this. It does not reassure her she will live. It only seeks revenge. Whose?

Catherine doesn't want revenge. She wants to open her eyes. But some part of Catherine must want revenge. Because it's the only feeling that runs through her body.

Is it possible for someone in a coma to lose her mind?

How did all of this happen? If only she could remember . . . .

Part I

THE SEED

Part I

THE SEED

Chapter One

At first, it was a slight stirring in the darkness. An adjustment of black on black. If the light was to be called goodness, then the Evil was there even before the darkness. It would have to be that way in order to measure the good. It could not even be called a force so many millions of years ago. The Evil was still too small, still too weak. A minute particle of the purest corruption.

New York City, 1984.

The wedding of Catherine Bellamy to Ian Price Bishop went off like a dream.

The joyous couple—she 25, he a decade older—exchanged nuptial vows at the Little Church Around The Corner, that venerable house of worship on Manhattan's Twenty-ninth Street, just off Fifth Avenue. The day was fair, a shimmering afternoon in late spring, the smell of lilacs an intoxicating presence. The groom, a man of brooding good looks and self-assurance, was imposing in his swallow-tailed coat, striped trousers, ascot and high silk hat. The bride— slender, dark haired and wide eyed—was a vision in white lace, fragile yet ethereal.

The minister, flown in first-class from Ian's hometown in the south of England, was a ruddy-faced prince of a man with pince-nez glasses. He was everyone's idea of a prototypical British vicar. The Bellamy clan, like the clergy-man, fresh from a transatlantic flight, were a sturdy familial group. They seemed a little bit above all the colonial goings-on, but were no less liked for that. Indeed they were even looked up to with admiration by the smattering of Catherine's acquaintances, who managed to fill only two pews in the stately old chapel. For the most part, those in attendance were friends of Ian's from the New York art world— painters, sculptors, photographers, designers, even a few fellow gallery owners whom the groom, in a gesture of benevolence, had deigned to invite.

During the ceremony, at the joining of hands, Ian had read from William Blake. Catherine, her voice halting in the midafternoon quiet, recited a poem by Emily Dickinson and was still.

Later, the wedding party, shepherded by Ian and his best man, Michael Spinoza, repaired en masse to a reception at the St. Regis. Catherine waited for Ian's summons—he was so good at taking care of people—before joining him in the limousine for the ride up to Central Park South.

That night was the most beautiful night of Catherine's 25 years on earth. She and Ian sipped champagne giddily, gorged themselves on Baked Alaska, danced until three in the hotel ballroom and made love in a bridal suite fit for king and queen.

The wedding went off like a fairy tale. Like a splendid, magical dream. But months later, there was another dream in Catherine's young mind.

A dream that wouldn't go away. . . .

"Mrs. Roberts, can you get that?"

The ringing telephone was barely audible in the Bishop living room, but its slight insistent sound had startled Catherine out of her reverie. Dressed casually at her marble-topped work desk, she focused her eyes once again on the photograph album, which had been occupying her attention earlier. It was a lavish volume of pictures and souvenirs commemorating Catherine and Ian's wedding. She had been meticulously captioning the photos with pen-and-ink calligraphy when she had drifted off into introspection 20 minutes earlier.

Animus

Catherine stood up. She stretched her limbs and walked dreamily to the window that offered a striking panorama of the New York skyline. Outside, the first shades of night were beginning to march across the expanse of Central Park.

The Bishop living room was severely modern in design, emphasized in glass, chrome and marble. Several minimalist paintings hung on the walls. The chairs and sofas were of black leather, in marked contrast to the white rug underfoot. There was a coldness about the room; it hardly invited one to feel at home. At least, that had been Catherine's impression upon first seeing Ian's design. But then Ian knew so much more about such things. Surely, she would get used to the room, someday.

Mrs. Roberts, the housekeeper, appeared in the doorway. She was an elderly woman—Catherine suspected she was pushing 80—but she moved with a spunkiness that belied her advanced years.

"Mrs. Bishop, it's your husband," the old woman announced in her clipped English accent.

"Thanks, I'll take it in here."

Catherine hurried to the glass coffee table and picked up the receiver. "Ian?"

As soon as she heard his voice, Catherine pictured her husband in his art gallery. He would be dressed impeccably in a three-piece pinstripe suit. The gallery was stark with a minimum of furnishings. The paintings on the walls revealed sharp symmetrical lines in perfect accord with the grave modern decor of the rooms. Ian's voice on the other end of the line was cultured and resonant.

"Do you know Edwardo's?" he asked. "We have reservations in a half hour."

Catherine fluttered involuntarily. "Ian, you always do this. I just put a roast in the oven."

"You mean Mrs. Roberts put a roast in the oven. Well, have her take the bloody thing out."

"I really don't feel like going out," Catherine protested. "I'm tired."

"You're tired? I've been working all day. I'll see you at the bar."

Ian hung up the phone.

Catherine had never been to Edwardo's, but that was often the case when Ian suggested that they meet at a restaurant. Ian was a collector of restaurants. Moreover, he had an uncanny knack for knowing exactly when they were about to become fashionable. Except for the stalwarts—places like Lutece, La Cote Basque and The Palm—Ian had little patience for traditional restaurants. Nor was he interested in the splashy newcomers that threw open their doors with great fanfare only to disappear in ignominy a few months later. Ian preferred to catch an on-the-rise restaurant just as it was nearing the curve of acceptance, and his skill at foretelling that evanescent frisson of societal buzz was akin to his highly touted ability to book an up-and-coming artist before the major galleries even knew that person existed. Of course, once a restaurant caught on, it was only a matter of time before Ian dropped it in favor of someplace else.

Nestled a few doors from Park Avenue in the East 50s, Edwardo's was a posh seafood establishment decorated in lush blues and greens. Its tables were mirror topped. Its booths were of black leather. Its maitre d' still had a rein on his surliness.

"Tell me about your day," Ian said. His tone was almost like a father's to his little girl. He and Catherine were ensconced in the prestigious corner booth. Catherine wore a black crepe dress that accentuated her pale complexion.

"I got an order for some dolls," Catherine said, trying desperately to mute the recitative lilt to her voice. "Two dozen. A store on Martha's Vineyard."

"That will bring in a few dollars."

"And I started on the scrapbook."

Ian laughed mirthlessly. "That's nice. It's only been six months."

"I know. I'm terrible. We've been married for six months." Catherine hesitated. "I've been so happy."

Ian leaned forward. His eyes traveled slowly across Catherine's face. After a moment, he sat back against the leather. "You don't look well," he noted.

"I had trouble sleeping last night," Catherine confessed.

Ian sipped his dry martini. His steel-gray eyes studied her. "Really?"

"I had a bad dream. It's the third time this week I've had the same nightmare. It was about my father. He was slashing himself with the razor. I was back in the house. In Nantucket. I was a little girl again. There was so much blood—it was horrible. I couldn't get back to sleep."

Ian's handsome face creased into a frown. "Your father didn't slash himself. He fell on the razor. It was an accident. You know that."

"It was real," Catherine continued, as if her husband hadn't spoken. "I could see the blood coming out of his face."

Ian glanced around the restaurant. "Catherine, for God's sake," he muttered.

Catherine lowered her voice. "I'm sorry." She paused. "Don't you ever have bad dreams?"

Ian knotted his brows. It was a habit he had when a question came his way that he considered serious.

"Yes," he said after a moment, "but I don't dwell on them. If you keep thinking about nightmares, you'll keep having them."

"I'm not dwelling on it. You said I didn't look well. I'm telling you the reason."

Ian waved a hand dismissively. "You should go to bed early tonight. If you have trouble sleeping, take a pill."

Catherine gazed past Ian at a line on the wall where blue and green met in a touch of turquoise.

"I hope that dream doesn't come back," she said, remembering to keep her voice soft for her husband.

Later that night, Catherine and Ian were side by side in their four-poster bed. Catherine was propped up against some overstuffed pillows, reading a paperback novel. Ian stared fixedly at the ceiling.

"Have you thought about it?" Ian asked.

"Ian, I don't want to have a baby. It's too soon."

"It's not too soon. It might do you good."

"We've got time."

"It's your mother, isn't it? You're afraid you'll die giving birth too?"

Catherine didn't answer.

Chapter Two

Once again a little, chestnut-haired girl, Catherine walks on tiptoes through the hallway. In her hand, she holds a crayon. As she walks, the crayon makes strokes against the wall.

Suddenly, Catherine turns. Different colored party balloons begin popping, making gunshot-type noises. She is afraid. But still she continues marking the wall with the crayon. And going a step closer. And closer. . . .

She is in the doorway. She smiles. It's her father. Surely nothing could hurt her now.

But, wait, something is wrong.

There is blood pouring from his cheek. He drops something onto the tiled floor and the floor becomes claylike and pliable. Crayons start to sprout from in between the tiled floor.

Catherine's father slumps down. And the crayons seem to go right through his body. No longer just red crayons now. All different colors. Matching the balloons that are still bursting.

A woman approaches. Catherine can't make out her face. The woman looks very kind. She is very beautiful. She puts her hand out to touch Catherine. But something happens. The woman's hand turns into . . . a razor. And it begins to slash at her own face.

Catherine cannot seem to turn around and run away. The woman begins to make slashing marks with the razor. From her neck down. When she reaches Catherine's stomach, she cuts it from side to side. As her stomach opens up, Catherine screams in horror, and suddenly a little baby is lying there.

The woman looks at Catherine and starts to laugh.

Catherine opens her mouth and screams. She doesn't stop screaming. A trickle of urine snakes down her leg.

Catherine Bishop shot up in bed. Her own scream was what caused her to get up.

Beside her, Ian was instantly awake. He put his arm around Catherine, trying to comfort her.

But Catherine was too hysterical.

"It was the same dream," she cried.

As she sobbed, Ian held her. His concern seemed mixed with vexation.

31

* * *

Morning sunlight shone steadfastly through the windows of the Bishop kitchen, a large, ultramodern room with all the latest conveniences. Mrs. Roberts stood at the central counter, mixing a health drink in a blender.

A short time earlier, the housekeeper had heard Catherine moving about in the master bedroom. Poor girl, Mrs. Roberts thought, she'd had a rough night. Sometime after three in the morning, the housekeeper—a lifelong light sleeper—had awakened. In robe and curlers, she'd tiptoed down the hall and listened outside the main bedroom. Catherine's muffled crying had come from within. It was not the first time, of late, the elderly woman had heard Mrs. Bishop weeping in the dark of the night.

Catherine, looking adrift in her pale blue terry-cloth robe, appeared in the kitchen doorway. She seemed particularly haggard in the harsh glare of the room's fluorescent lights.

"When did Ian leave?" Catherine asked sleepily.

Mrs. Roberts spoke above the noise of the blender. "About nine. He said I should let you sleep."

The housekeeper turned off the blender and poured the health drink into a large tumbler.

"What's that?" Catherine asked.

"Papaya, yogurt, honey, wheat germ—this will perk you up."

32

Catherine looked dubious. "I'm supposed to drink that?"

"You don't have to, but you look like you could use a lift."

Catherine sank wearily onto a bar stool at the counter. "I was up most of the night."

"Indeed."

Catherine sampled the health concoction. "This is good. It sounded weird, but it's good."

"I heard you last night," Mrs. Roberts said. "You nearly scared me to death."

"I'm sorry if I woke you. I've been having bad dreams."

"A young girl like you, a new bride—you shouldn't be having bad dreams. What did you dream?"

"It wasn't important."

"They say if you talk about a nightmare in the morning, it'll go away."

Catherine finished the health drink and sighed. "I wish it was that easy."

Ian Bishop's art gallery, located on Madison Avenue in the low 60s, was, if anything, even more streamlined than the Bishop apartment. Though Ian disdained the term post-modern, the spacious second-floor rooms positively reeked of that designation, with everything from the lighting to the angled walls to the exhibits themselves representing a delicious irony as a comment on all that had gone before in the art world.

Ian was supervising the arrangement of paintings for a new show. Helping him was the gallery manager Lisa Gamble, an attractive, highly efficient woman of about 27. The show was an exhibit of post-modern art, the geometrical lines of which were in harmony with the stark, even humorous decor of the room. Ian directed the arrangement with a cold, precise eye for form and detail.

"Lisa," Ian said, indicating a painting of a square grapefruit, "this one goes over there."

Lisa bit a fingernail doubtfully. "Are you sure?"

"The light. Don't you see the difference?"

Lisa considered the way the gelled track light above was glinting off the canvas. "I do see," she said, giving Ian an almost worshipful smile.

Ian nodded his approval. "Did you finish the invitations?" he asked.

"The press mailing went out this morning. I'm still working on the V.I.P. list. The *Times* is sending a reporter from the society section."

"Good. I want this opening to be something special."

"I ordered the champagne. Ten cases."

Ian hung another picture on the wall. It was a sombre black canvas that looked somewhat foreboding. Lisa stepped back and studied it for a minute.

"My, my," she said, finally. "That's pretty morbid. It looks like pure evil."

Ian's quick grin exposed his gleaming teeth.

"I should raise the price. People are fascinated by evil."

Catherine's studio was remarkably friendly, so warm in comparison to the rest of her apartment. Though a bit dusty and cluttered, it reflected warmth and creativity. Antique furniture, polished to a sheen, surrounded a large work table.

Catherine went to the old-fashioned coatrack and found her smock. She put it on and tied it in the back. Then she faced her work space. There were at least a dozen dolls' heads on the table in various stages of makeup. Some smiled at her with bright red lips, but saw her through eyeless lids. Some had no mouth. Some had no nose.

She went to one of the dolls' heads. She studied it for a moment. She picked up a pen-and-ink drawing that was on her bulletin board. The sketch was of a cheerful beautiful smiling little boy's face. Catherine began to mix paints.

Expertly, she started painting the doll's face to match the pen-and-ink sketch.

Something was wrong.

Catherine began to frown. The mouth. Something was not right with the mouth. The lips pointed down. Where was the smile? What was happening to her? Why couldn't she stop?

She moved away from the mouth and went back to drawing the eyes. As the paint began to dry around the dark eyes, she noticed a malevolent quality. How could this be happening? She had done this a hundred times before. The doll was beginning to take on a life of its own.

Frightened, she put it down. She stared at it for a moment. There was something about it, something familiar. Something very eerily familiar.

Catherine didn't know how long she sat there staring at the doll's head. But suddenly the slivers of light that poured through the window were gone. Somehow, night had taken over. And the warm friendly room took on another feeling. She had to get out of there. . . .

She threw her smock off and ran out of the room, slamming the door behind her. What was happening to her? Why was she feeling like this?

How could she be afraid of something she was creating?

"Is this the Rembrandt exhibit?"

Ian and Lisa looked up from their gallery preparations. A tall, dark-haired man of about 35, dressed neatly in a blue suit, was speaking into the microphone at the glass partition that led into the studio. Seeing his best friend Michael Spinoza, Ian brightened.

"We don't carry those old-timers," Ian shouted. He buzzed Michael into the studio.

"I can see that," Michael remarked, eyeing the macabre art works Ian and Lisa had been hanging.

Ian came forward, taking Lisa's hand. "I don't think you two have met. Lisa Gamble, my new manager. Michael Spinoza. Michael is my lawyer."

Michael smiled at the young woman. "How do you put up with this guy? Look at this stuff. What you need in here are some Monets, Renoirs, Vermeers. The Old Masters."

Ian gave Lisa a wry smile. "Michael has difficulty adjusting to the twentieth century."

"Don't we all?" Lisa chirped.

"Not Ian," Michael said. "He seems perfectly at home in the modern world."

Ian rubbed his hands together vigorously. "And ready for the future."

Two hours later, Ian and Michael were just finishing lunch at L'Autre, an obscure French restaurant near the United Nations that Ian had been keeping his eye on for several months. Overpriced and underdecorated, the low-ceilinged room looked like something out of Albert Camus. Even the waiters in their dark, loose-fitting garments seemed to be living some existential nightmare.

Over espresso, served in ice-cream-parlor glasses decorated with a variation on Munch's *The Scream*, Michael spread some legal papers on the table. Ian examined them.

"Have you ever seen the house?" Michael asked.

"I've never been to Nantucket," Ian replied quietly.

Michael pointed to one of the documents. "Well, as of Catherine's twenty-fifth birthday, it's hers free and clear."

Ian's eyes narrowed. "What about her father?"

"He's in Switzerland. He has nothing to say about this. Catherine's mother had it in her will. It's ironclad."

Ian sipped his espresso. "I wonder how Catherine will feel, going back there after all these years."

"That's where the accident happened, isn't it?"

"Yes. And the first thing I want to do is redecorate the whole place. I don't want Catherine to be reminded of her childhood."

"Just being there is going to remind her. Nantucket hasn't changed that much. Do you think it's a good idea taking her back there?"

"Why do you ask that?"

Michael looked away from Ian's penetrating stare. "You know how Catherine is. Her imagination—"

"It's overactive," Ian interrupted. "To say the least. She's been dreaming about the accident. I think inheriting the house has brought it all back to her."

"What kind of dreams?"

"Bad ones. She's been having them all week. Last night, she woke up screaming. It took her hours to get back to sleep. She's keeping *me* awake. Catherine is currently very . . . troubled. I'm even considering getting professional help for her."

"You mean a psychiatrist?"

Ian nodded. "Do you know one? A good one?"

Michael considered for a moment. "One of my clients is a Jungian psychologist."

Ian took a pen from his jacket. "What's his name?"

"Her name," Michael said, unable to resist a smile, "is Janet Parker. She's a friend. She might be able to help. Have you talked to Catherine about this?"

Ian snapped his fingers for the check at a waiter who looked like an update of Edgar Allan Poe.

"Not yet," Ian said, "but she'll do what's best for her. She's married now. She has got to get her act together. If we're ever going to have a family, Catherine has got to stop acting like a child herself."

Coming out into the bright sunlight, after the gloomy atmosphere of L'Autre, both men blinked as if emerging into a new landscape.

"I hope you haven't forgotten the reunion party," Michael said.

"What night is it?"

"Next Friday."

Ian pondered. "That will be two days after

the opening. I should have recovered. I'll be there."

"That's what you've said for the last three years."

"Michael, I will be there. I will meet you after work. We'll have a drink. We'll go to the party together. And you'll call the lady shrink?"

Chapter Three

Michael and Laura Spinoza lived in a comfortable five-room apartment on East Eighty-first Street, between Second and Third Avenue. For Michael, who had grown up in a tenement in Little Italy, it represented a vindication of a childhood lived on the edge of poverty, and he relished the modest luxuriousness of his adult surroundings. Not that he was one to think only of himself, or only of his lovely wife. Five years ago, settled into an attorney's niche that netted him six figures per year, he had moved his mother and father from their Elizabeth Street walk-up to a Tudor-style house in Brooklyn's Bensonhurst neighborhood, where they were securely settled. Family values were important to Michael and his parents' new home was small recompense to them for the many years they had sacrificed to send their only child through college and Columbia Law School. Michael was nothing if not a dutiful and grateful son.

The Spinoza living room was cozy, filled with plants and tastefully decorated with a white baby grand piano dominating one corner of the room. As the sun was setting, Laura Spinoza, a pretty woman of 29 with frizzy auburn hair and a slender figure, was seated at the piano, playing a Chopin etude. The front door opened noiselessly and Michael entered the room. He stood stock-still in admiration until Laura finished the piece. Michael always marveled at the facility and grace with which his wife approached the art of music. It was a joy for him to listen to her, captured there in apparent solitude, as her fingers glided effortlessly over the piano keys.

Laura looked up. She smiled. Michael came over and kissed her. "Chopin, right?"

"Very good," Laura said. "Would you believe I had a ten-year-old pupil in here today who played it letter-perfect?"

Michael set down his briefcase. "I need a drink. I had lunch with Ian today."

"You poor baby." Lisa laughed. "I'll fix it."

She got up and went over to the bar area in the opposite corner of the room. She took ice from a cooler and began preparing a drink. Michael sat down on the sofa.

"And how is Mr. Perfection?" Laura asked mischievously.

Michael grinned. "Ian's fine. Same as always. He wants Catherine to see a psychiatrist."

Laura snapped open a bottle of vodka. "Ian should see a psychiatrist. What's wrong with Catherine?"

"Bad dreams."

"If I was married to Ian, I'd be having bad dreams too."

"I referred him to Janet."

Laura splashed vodka into a glass. "I hope Catherine is all right. Maybe I should call her."

"Don't call her yet," Michael cautioned. "Ian hasn't told her."

"He's sending her to Janet and he hasn't even asked her?"

"You know Ian."

Laura stirred tomato juice into Michael's drink. She added Tabasco and stirred. She brought the drink to her husband on the sofa.

"Ian is prehistoric," Laura said. "He's like one of those cavemen dragging his wife around by her hair."

Michael chuckled at the image conjured up by her observation. "Now that you mention it, he did show up at the restaurant wearing an animal hide. But I made him check his spiked club at the door."

Laura didn't smile. "Catherine is fragile. Maybe Janet can do her some good."

"It can't hurt. It'll be good for Catherine to have someone objective to talk to."

"I know what you mean. Catherine talks to me, but only to a point. Then I can feel her closing up." Laura paused. "I just wonder about Ian's motives."

"His motives? I suppose he's concerned about Catherine."

Laura shook her head. "I think he's more concerned about other people. The way they look at his so-called perfect marriage."

Michael laughed. "You call that marriage perfect? He's a goddamn martinet and she's an eccentric dollmaker."

"You know what I'm talking about. The money. Ian married into a fortune. His family in England was middle-class at best. Catherine's money has put Ian on the map. And they're the original beautiful couple. Ian certainly doesn't want people thinking Catherine's not playing with a full deck."

"Janet's a good idea," Michael said. "Ian thinks he's doing the right thing."

Laura smiled wistfully. "Sure. Right for Ian."

A crisp autumnal breeze ruffled the foliage of Central Park; the city's playground was devoid of all but the most fearless and hapless occupants. The theaters and concert halls had emptied more than an hour earlier and the night's first confident solitude was shrouding the island.

Animus

Viewed from the Bishop apartment, the lights of Central Park's lamps were hooded jewels crisscrossing the expanse below like so many beaded beacons. The wind buffeted the apartment glass, rattling the classically quiet living room, where Bach's *Goldberg Variations* played unheard.

Down the hall, in Catherine's study, a half-formed face was alert. Its unformed ears were listening. . . .

"Oh, Ian, yes. . . . Oh, I love you. . . ."

On the four-poster bed that dominated the Bishops' master bedroom, moonlight flooded a tender scene. Naked, moaning in time with the insistent breeze, Catherine straddled her husband Ian, who was thrust deep inside her.

Ian's head rested regally on an extravagant down pillow, one of their wedding presents. His hands gently massaged his wife's exquisite breasts as she lowered her face to brush her lips against his.

"Oh, yes, Ian. Oh, God, yes. That feels so good. . . ."

Ian smiled through his wife's kisses. As he continued to arch upward, in time with Catherine's perfect internal workings, his hands moved in circles on her ripely hardened nipples, which for him represented the proof of her desire. His fingers moved upon them like electric sensors in the dark. Battery wires. Conductors. Catherine moaned again. Ian was conducting her. Catherine was an orchestra.

His own personal philharmonic.

And, only a corridor away, an unformed something waited in the wings. . . .

Later, Catherine, wearing a short negligee, brushed her hair before the vanity mirror. Ian lay under the blankets, thumbing contemptuously through a rival gallery's catalogue.

"I saw Michael today," Ian said, barely glancing over at his wife. "There's no problem about the house. As soon as you sign some papers, it's yours."

Catherine looked thoughtful, but made no reply. Her brush wound in and out of her long chestnut hair.

"I guess it'll be strange for you," Ian continued. "It's been a long time."

"Seventeen years," Catherine replied dreamily. "Nantucket is so beautiful, Ian. I can't wait to show you the whole island."

"You want to go back?"

"There are so many special places," Catherine said, getting enthusiastic. "Little coves and beaches. Wait till you see the house! It's almost magical."

Ian looked surprised. "I thought the house upset you."

Catherine put down her brush. "The house doesn't upset me. Just what happened to my father."

"I told Michael about your dreams. He thinks it's not a good idea for you to go back there."

Animus

Catherine turned to her husband in disbelief. "You told Michael about my dreams?"

"Catherine, I'm worried about you. Come over here. I want to tell you something."

Catherine got up tentatively and approached the bed. She sat on the edge.

"You don't want to keep having those dreams, do you?" Ian's voice had turned silken.

"No. What are you getting at?"

Ian put an arm on her shoulder. "Michael has a friend. She's a psychologist. I called her today. Her schedule is very tight, but she can see you day after tomorrow."

Catherine looked stunned. "Ian, what are you doing? I don't need a psychologist. I won't go!"

"You will go. It's for your own good."

"I went for seven years after my father hurt himself. It didn't do me any good!"

"This is different. You're a grown woman. You're married now. You have responsibilities. You owe it to yourself. You owe it to me."

Catherine slid away from Ian's grasp. Tears welled in her large hazel eyes.

"I won't go! I hate the idea of people probing around in my head. All the questions. Telling intimate thoughts to strangers. Seven years was enough. I couldn't stand to go through all that again."

"Listen to what you sound like. I simply made one appointment. I'm only asking you to meet the woman. Is that unreasonable?"

Ed Kelleher & Harriette Vidal

Catherine's tears coursed down her face. "Ian, I can't."

"Is that unreasonable?" Ian repeated, his voice turning darker. "She's one of Michael's closest friends. I wouldn't ask you if I didn't think it could help."

Catherine pulled farther away. "Help? I don't need help. . . ." Her voice trailed off. Her eyes widened. "Do I?"

48

Chapter Four

The Evil was patient. Infinitely patient. As the elements formed and the universe expanded, the malignant morsel grew. Almost imperceptibly in the beginning, and then like a cancerous growth, spreading along with the matter. The Evil was crafty. It stayed in the background. It knew once the other elements sensed its presence, they would try to destroy it. And try they did. But by then it was too late.

"My father was scary," Catherine said. "I think I've been afraid of him for as long as I can remember. He was away a lot. He's in the shipping business. When he was away, I missed him. But when he was home, I was terrified. I remember one time on Nantucket, I made up

49

a song. I thought he'd like it. I thought I could make him love me."

"Go on, Catherine."

Dr. Janet Parker, an attractive, stylishly dressed woman in her late 30s, studied the hesitancy on the face of her newest patient. The two women sat across from each other in comfortable leather armchairs. The office was warm, inviting, filled with contemporary furnishings. Several David Hockney prints hung on the wall, adding further brightness to the surroundings. From seven floors below, on West End Avenue, sounds of traffic occasionally drifted through the old-fashioned casement windows, which looked out on the Hudson River.

"I guess I was eight years old," Catherine continued, closing her eyes to concentrate. "I was sitting on the porch swing. I'd found this little flute at the five and ten. I was teaching myself to play 'Greensleeves.' My father was in the den. I suppose he was trying to work. But I wasn't playing very loud. Suddenly, he just burst through the screen door. His face was all red. He could barely speak. It was like he was in a rage."

"Do you remember what he said?"

"Yes," Catherine replied. "I remember exactly what he said like it was yesterday."

"Tell me."

Catherine's lip trembled. "It was more like a bellow. He said: 'I'm trying to work. You've been playing that damn flute for an hour. It's the same thing over and over. It's driving me crazy.' "

"Go on," Janet suggested gently.

"Well, he grabbed the flute out of my hand. It was rough, the way he did it. He glared at me. I was frightened. He said: 'I'll hold on to this. You go to your room. If you can't play the flute without bothering people, you don't deserve to have it.' "

Dr. Parker waited to see if Catherine would continue. Instead, the room grew silent, save for the cry of seagulls high above the Hudson.

"What about your mother?"

"She died—giving birth to me." Catherine hesitated. "Sometimes, I think my father blamed me for her death."

"That's not really that unusual," Janet observed kindly, "especially in cases where the father has a very strong sense of order."

"My father had that all right. He kept everything in its place—including me."

"Were you very lonely?"

"Yes. I read a lot. I had a pretty healthy imagination. I still do."

"This dream about your father's injury—why do you think you've suddenly started having it?"

Catherine turned slightly to meet the psychologist's eyes head-on.

"I don't know. I was hoping you could tell me."

"Mr. Bishop mentioned that you were in therapy before."

"Until I was fifteen. I went away to school and I just never continued the sessions. I'm not sure they did that much good anyway."

"How do you mean?"

Catherine cleared her throat. "I'm still not convinced my father didn't cut himself intentionally."

"In the dream, do you feel yourself wishing he would hurt himself?"

"I'm not sure," Catherine said defensively.

"You and your husband are newlyweds, aren't you?"

"Yes. Why?"

Janet Parker extended a warm smile. "Sometimes when a person's lifestyle changes—through marriage, a new home, whatever—that person subconsciously goes back to childhood, looking for a simpler, more familiar world. Because your childhood included such an obviously traumatic experience—your father's injury—your subconscious could be reliving that trauma."

"Through the dream," Catherine said.

"Exactly."

"But why is it so real?"

Catherine had no memory of going back into the studio. Everything was as she had left it. She picked up the discarded smock from the floor and tied it.

She looked at her supplies. Some of the paint had dried up; she hadn't covered it in her haste to leave. That wasn't like her. She was usually very careful about this.

She ignored the boy's face that she had been working on. Instead, she went to another doll. She picked it up and tried painting eyes.

Something would not let her.

This is ridiculous, she thought. What's the matter with me?

She could feel something staring at her. Something dark. Something behind her.

Catherine whirled around, dropping the doll's head to the floor. She stared directly into the boy doll's malevolent grin. But wait. She had painted a frown on its face. Why were the lips turned up? What was happening? When had she done that?

Strangely enough, though the doll's head had an evil quality to it, there was something compelling about it. Catherine began to concentrate. Again the familiar feeling. She knew that face. Where had she seen it before?

Slowly, she went to the doll's head. She picked it up tenderly. It almost seemed to smile wider as she gazed into its eyes. Lovingly, she picked up a brush and daubed in some paint. She was no longer afraid. Sweat beaded on her upper lip.

Catherine worked far into the night. At least, she thought she did. She lost all sense of time. As she skillfully applied paint, the doll's head slowly began to take shape—and life.

Chapter Five

The Bishop dining room maintained the apartment's modern decor. It was dominated by a large glass table that was surrounded by chrome-frame chairs. A crystal chandelier hung over Ian and Catherine as they sat across from each other that evening. Mrs. Roberts served them noiselessly.

"I was nervous at first," Catherine said. "But Janet is really a nice person."

Ian smiled paternally. "Oh, so it's Janet already. You two really got along."

Catherine looked thoughtful. "She says I should think of our meetings as just friendly discussions. I like that."

"I told you she was good."

"What do you know about her?"

"Only what Michael told me," Ian replied. "She's thirty-eight. She's written two books on Jungian psychology. She's recently divorced. And Michael swears by her."

"What did her husband do?"

"I'm not sure. I think he was a teacher."

"Any children?"

"No. Michael said they didn't want any."

Catherine raised an eyebrow. "Oh, really. That's interesting."

"More squash, Mr. Bishop?" the housekeeper interrupted.

Ian nodded. Mrs. Roberts spooned some squash onto his plate. The old woman glanced at Catherine, who shook her head no. Mrs. Roberts looked disapproving as she started off toward the kitchen, her ears still perked for the dinner conversation.

Ian waited until the housekeeper was gone. "So you felt comfortable?" he continued.

"Yes," Catherine responded. "I felt like I was talking to a friend."

Ian nibbled his squash. "I told you. You should listen to me more often."

The tunnel is dark and ominous. Again, clay-like walls, pulsating with a life of their own.

The young Catherine, dressed in a summer frock, walks haltingly down the length of the tunnel. Her feet barely touch the ground. It is almost as if she is floating. She hurries, because at the end of the tunnel there is the much-needed sunlight.

Eight-year-old Catherine emerges from the tunnel. The ankle-high grass leaves dew marks on her socks. She loves the feeling. It tickles her. She skips and finally comes to a large rock. She sits down. It is all beautiful there.

Flowers of all different colors bloom around her. And even though it is a dream, she can smell their scent.

She takes out a large pad and a pencil. Catherine begins to draw.

She cocks her head to one side and stares at the little boy who sits before her.

"Now sit still, Bobo. I can't draw you if you don't sit still."

She pauses.

"That's better. I'm so glad you wore your nice new shirt. How did you know I had that color red? Oh, Bobo, you know everything." The little girl laughs and it sounds like a melody. "What did you say?" She listens for an answer. "Yes, Bobo, after I finish the drawing, we can play on the swing. Now please sit still. . . ."

Slowly, magically, facial features begin to take shape on Catherine's pad. As she draws, she hums a lovely melody. It sounds very much like the one she knows how to play on the flute.

She draws a red shirt and colors it in. She adds finishing touches to the hair. She sits back, proud of her work.

It took a moment for Catherine to realize that she was no longer in her bed.

Instead, she was standing in the doorway of her studio. She hugged herself with her arms. She was dressed only in a short nightie. What was she doing there? She smiled. Must have been dreaming.

Suddenly, as if she zoomed in with a fish-eye lens, her eyes went directly to the doll's head she had been painting. Catherine gasped.

It was her dream. It was the sketch in her dream. The doll's head was the same as the sketch in the dream she had just woken from.

At first, Catherine was horrified. Something was happening to her. Something she could not explain and could not talk to anyone about. But then it began to fall together, piece by piece. As if the puzzle in her mind were shaping itself the same way she shaped the doll's head, it all fell together. Catherine smiled.

There was nothing to be afraid of. She would probably not have to be afraid ever again.

He was back.

Somehow, Bobo was back—and he was real.

Catherine began to hum a melody. It was vaguely familiar to her. But she wasn't sure where it came from.

Chapter Six

"Ian, when you were a child, did you ever have an imaginary playmate?"

It was 8:30 the following morning. Catherine perched at the kitchen table, dressed in a t-shirt and jeans. Ian, dressed and ready for work, was picking at his toast while finishing his coffee.

"No, why?" Ian replied coldly.

Catherine pressed on, ignoring his mood. "You never spoke to someone that no one else could see?"

"Absolutely not." Ian paused. "Okay, Catherine, what is it?"

"You know that nightmare? I don't think I'll be having it anymore. I had a different dream last night. I think I know what I've been trying to do subconsciously. Get in touch with Bobo."

"Bobo?"

Catherine smiled. "My playmate."

"Your imaginary playmate," Ian said, correcting her.

Catherine looked away. "Well, to me he was real. He was always there when I needed him. He loved me."

Ian crushed a piece of toast between his fingers. "Isn't that a bit ridiculous?"

"When I was little, I was very lonely. Bobo was my friend. He went away after my father hurt himself. He was away a long time—ever since I was eight years old. Now I feel like he's coming back through my dreams. It's as if he can tell that I need him."

Ian stood up. He looked incredulous. "This is too nuts. I've got to go to work."

Catherine reached for his arm. "Don't go. Not yet. This is important."

Ian looked down at his wife. "You're twenty-five years old. You're a married woman and you have an imaginary playmate. You tell me that's important. Goddamn it, Catherine, get a grip on yourself. If anyone could hear you talking like this, they'd think you were crazy!"

Catherine withdrew from his words. Her voice became softer. "I'm not crazy. Bobo is back. He's back to help me. He's back because I need him."

"You need him? What in God's name for?"

"Dr. Parker says that when a person's lifestyle changes, they can go back subconsciously to their childhood. Bobo was an important part of my childhood."

"And should remain in your childhood. I didn't marry you so I could share you with an imaginary playmate."

"Ian."

"I don't want to hear any more about Bobo. You got that? Grow up."

Ian stormed out of the room. A moment later, the front door slammed.

Catherine walked into the hallway and stood there. A feeling of dread crept over her. Suddenly, she turned. Her eyes zoomed to the open door of her studio, right to the boy doll.

Catherine was startled. She rubbed her eyes. For a moment, she thought she saw a tear falling from the corner of the doll's eye. She shook her head, tried to clear her vision. Very slowly, she walked to the room.

Tentatively, she went closer to inspect the doll. She reached out to touch its face. She scolded herself. Of course there was no tear. It was just a doll. It wasn't real. But, still. . . .

It was something. She felt it. Very quietly, her voice barely a whisper, she called, "Bobo?"

Mrs. Roberts trudged along the street, pushing a shopping cart with supplies from Gristede's. There was a smug smile on her face. The checkout girl had tried to tell her that her coupons for tapioca had expired the previous day, but Mrs. Roberts had protested to the supermarket manager, who had ruled in her behalf. Those little hussies at the checkout counters, Mrs. Roberts sniffed, all they cared about was chatting with one another about their lazy boyfriends, who didn't have jobs at all.

The doorman nodded at Mrs. Roberts as she approached the building. She gave him a grim smile as he held the door for her and her cart.

Upstairs, in the kitchen, Mrs. Roberts un-packed the grocery bags. She put them on the counter and walked toward the hallway. She was just taking off her trenchcoat. . . .

What on earth was that?

It sounded like muffled laughter. Strange laughter. The housekeeper frowned. She went down the hall and stopped outside the closed door of Catherine's studio. She put an ear to the door and listened.

Catherine's voice came from inside. "I told Ian about you." There was a giggle. "He thinks I'm bananas. I can't believe you're back. Bobo, I'm so glad to see you! You're all grown up. Just like me. And you're so handsome." There was a pause. "Do you really think I'm beautiful? Thank you."

Curiosity getting the better of her, Mrs. Roberts cautiously turned the doorknob. She opened the door a crack, just enough to see inside.

Catherine was sitting in her rocking chair, her head thrown back, her chestnut hair in cascades to her neck. She stared up at the ceiling. Across the room, the malevolent boy doll was a strong presence. His features had been finished.

Mrs. Roberts felt a pang of dread travel along her spine. She could see there was no one else in the room.

Yet Catherine spoke. Dreamily.

"Thank you for coming back. You always know when I want you."

Uncomfortable and frightened, the housekeeper noiselessly closed the door.

Chapter Seven

The Evil became an entity separate from the life forces. Once that happened, it was just a matter of time before it found a place to nest. It did not matter that this would take millions of years. The Evil had all the time in the world. It would make its home thousands of times over.

Lisa Gamble, the manager of Ian's art gallery, was a woman who thrived on work. And with the opening of the gallery's new show only two nights away, that was exactly what she was faced with.

Dressed severely in black, her only jewelry a chunky Sudanese bracelet she'd had since her freshman year at Swarthmore, Lisa perched in the corner of her cubicle at the back end of the gallery, her shoeless feet tucked under her on a gigantic black cushion left over from a 1983 exhibit called *Stark What?*.

It was late morning. The air conditioner hummed efficiently nearby. Looking out the window onto Madison Avenue, Lisa could tell that the Indian summer heat had kicked in. The pedestrians on the sidewalk plodded along helplessly, their bodies sagging from the ravages of another New York summer that refused to die, their eyes sometimes darting heavenward as if some god could alleviate their sweat and misery.

Lisa consulted her Filofax, that trusted computerized personal organizer without which her life could not go on. She smiled contentedly. Not even eleven A.M. and she was already ahead of the rigorous schedule she had set for herself. It paid to come to work early. Lisa had been in the gallery since 6:30, a full two hours before Ian even showed up. Hours of quiet, before the rat race began—that was when she could really work. That was how she got things done. It was the way she got the reputation for being a woman who thrived on work.

She fingered the cushion beneath her. The *Stark What?* exhibit had been the first one she'd seen at Ian's gallery. Lisa had been fresh from a year's tour of Europe, trudging the art history paths, falling in love with a professor who was something of an art forger (concentrating on Klee), waiting for something significant to happen with her life.

But it hadn't happened overnight. *Stark What?* had opened up something in Lisa. Although some of the critics dismissed it as just another drab way station on the relentless journey of the minimalists, Lisa recognized that, in its juxtaposition of three painters from Scandinavia, it was more than the sum of its meager parts. The way the solid grays and blacks of one artist were complemented by the bull's-eye figures of the second and the trompe l'oeil playfulness of the third impressed her. She realized the overwhelming presence of Ian Bishop's personality in the complete harmony that the trio of artists—who hadn't even met before the exhibit—seemed to express. Leaving the gallery that day, Lisa had set her professional cap for the man she considered an artist of presentation—a con man, perhaps, to his detractors—who functioned in the art world much as a great choreographer did in dance.

Lisa had bided her time. But she went back to *Stark What?* three more times. She wore the same clothes on each occasion, the better to be noticed by Ian Bishop. Her strategy paid off. On the third visit—just as she had been about to leave—she felt Ian's piercing steel-gray eyes on her. She turned slightly, allowing her own eyes to skate casually across his face. Ian smiled. Another woman might have lingered. Lisa Gamble marched to the door and left, without a look back.

The rest had been easy, if arguably a little perverse.

Lisa waited months before returning to the gallery. This time, she dressed differently—in a short black dress and a single strand of pearls. Ian gazed at her the second she came in. Within minutes, he was pouring her some champagne in his private office. After one glass, he offered her an assistant manager's position at a humble salary. Lisa turned him down. Six months later, she returned in the simple black dress and pearls. Lisa knew Ian had recently lost his manager to a larger gallery. There was a new exhibit coming up. Lisa signed a contract that called for extremely generous wages.

Managing the Bishop Gallery proved to be that something significant Lisa had been searching for. Ian had taken a chance on her— a raw, overgrown kid who didn't know that much about art or business or, for that matter, organizing anything more complex than a ham and Swiss sandwich—because, as he explained later, he'd seen some untapped need, an unexpressed hunger to excel. Ian liked to tell that story. It made him seem like a prophet.

Remembering the afternoon two months earlier when she had first begun work in the gallery, Lisa smiled. Ian had been a prophet. Who else, at the beginning of the age of yuppies, would have hired a 27-year-old bum who looked like every other liberal arts major turned adult failure and dressed like black was the color of the universe? *Stark What?* indeed.

Lisa knew, of course, that Ian's actions had not been altruistic or even good business. He was sexually attracted to her. It was in his eyes, in the cool way he gazed at her whenever she approached. Lisa knew he wanted her. She also knew he'd never make the first move. That kind of man never did. Too cool. She wouldn't make the first move either. Not that she wasn't inclined. Ian was an extremely handsome man, and she occasionally speculated about the brutal things he would do to her in bed. Things she would enjoy with total compliance. But there was no future in that.

Lisa's eyes went to the window again. No let-up in the parade of sweat-drenched souls. Half a mile east and quite a few blocks north was her apartment—the one-bedroom flat she would one day purchase, thanks to her Bishop Gallery wages plus a tidy interest-free loan from Ian. Lisa smiled. She guessed that, right that moment, her 14-year-old tabby named Dietrich was flopped down on the living room window sill, surveying the backyard for errant pigeons and contemplating another nap. Dietrich had a good life; Lisa had had her since high school. But that wouldn't stop her from meowing fiercely the second she heard her master's key in the front door lock that night.

Lisa kept late hours. She rarely left the gallery before nine, and that was generally after Ian had gone home. Sometimes her friends wondered about her, suggesting that she lacked a social life. Lisa knew what that meant. They were wondering why she didn't have a man. Actually, there had been four or five since she'd arrived in New York. But they hadn't lasted. Most men Lisa's age or older were the kind who stuck around a girl until they felt threatened by a commitment. Lisa offered no such threat—the mere thought of a commitment gave her the cold sweats, plus it was so boring. Once the guys she went out with suspected her true feelings, they lingered only for a few more encounters, then disappeared conveniently from her life. Men—she could never figure them. But God knew they could sometimes be handy—Lisa grinned mischievously at the thought—and they could be amusing, up to a point.

Then, of course, there was Ian. . . .

Lisa's thoughts were interrupted by Ian's voice as he approached her corner of the gallery.

"Lisa, did you happen to call. . . . "

Lisa smiled, reading his mind. "The car service?"

Ian paused in midstep. His gallery manager's prescience had, for some time, ceased to astonish him, but he still found it a source of delight.

"I ordered you a limousine for the opening," Lisa said. "Your favorite driver."

"Melissa?"

"Exactly." Melissa was a petite redhead with a trim, hard beauty.

Ian nodded with satisfaction. "What about dinner?"

"I made reservations at Elaine's. Six people at eleven o'clock."

"Good." Ian was staring at something. A morbid death painting that was leaning against the wall, awaiting its mounting for the exhibit. "I want that night to be perfect."

Lisa laughed casually. "Of course it will be perfect."

Ian didn't smile. He continued to stare at the grotesque canvas. He seemed fascinated by it. He turned and walked away. Under his breath, out of Lisa's earshot, he spoke in an icy, whispery tone.

"Perfect? It had better be perfect . . . Catherine."

Chapter Eight

Later that same day, Catherine opened her front door and welcomed her friend Laura Spinoza.

"What a nice surprise."

The two women hugged. Laura held up a shopping bag. "I was buying sheet music. I was two blocks away."

Catherine grinned, leading her down the hallway toward the living room. "A shopping bag full of sheet music?"

"I got you a present at Bloomingdale's. Something that's you. I couldn't resist."

Laura took off her straw fedora. As if out of nowhere, Mrs. Roberts appeared to take it from her hand.

"Hello, Mrs. Spinoza," the old housekeeper said gravely, giving the young woman a cool, cautious look. "Can I get you something?"

"No, I can only stay a minute."

"Don't be silly," Catherine protested. "You've been walking around. It's hot outside—that's what I heard anyway. Have a soda or something."

"Maybe half an iced tea," Laura said.

As if issued an order, Mrs. Roberts exited toward the kitchen. Catherine and Laura went into the living room and Laura took a package from her shopping bag. She handed the gaily wrapped gift to Catherine, who opened it excitedly. Inside was a pop-art necklace featuring little doll figures.

"It's great," Catherine said enthusiastically.

Laura smiled. "I thought of you right away."

Catherine kissed her on the cheek. As Laura fastened the necklace for her, Catherine admired herself in the mirror. The tiny doll figures seemed to dance and writhe on her neck as she moved back and forth before the glass.

"How's the doll business?" Laura asked.

"Not bad. I'm doing some clowns for The Magnificent Doll. You know that store on Sixtieth Street?"

"Sure. I just walked by it."

"It's run by a couple from Warsaw. Agnieszka and Zbigniew. They've been together for fifty years but they're not married. Agnieszka claims she's related to the Polish royal family. Zbigniew is a peasant and proud of it. Agnieszka designs dolls and Zbigniew constructs them. Of course, they also buy from outside artists, which is where I come in."

"I love when you tell stories."

"I'm not making this up, Laura."

Mrs. Roberts returned with a tray. She served Laura her iced tea.

"I hear you met our friend Janet," Laura offered, sipping her drink.

Mrs. Roberts had started for the kitchen, but lingered in the doorway, hoping to pick up on some intriguing gossip. Catherine glanced at her.

"That'll be all, Mrs. Roberts."

Looking more than a little chagrined, the housekeeper marched off.

Catherine waited until the old woman's footsteps faded. "I had one session with Janet and I liked her very much."

"I thought you would," Laura said.

The two women chatted for more than an hour, during which time Laura began to feel relaxed about what she thought of as the whole problem with Janet.

Ever since Michael had first told her that Ian was sending Catherine to the psychologist without even conferring with his wife on the matter, Laura had felt vaguely guilty. She knew it had been nothing of her doing, yet she resented Ian's arrogance and wondered if Catherine would resist Dr. Parker and follow a trail of blame to the Spinozas. For a while,

Laura had even been slightly peeved at her own husband, feeling that Michael had overstepped his bounds by suggesting that Catherine visit Janet. Before long, however, she had realized that was silly. Michael had only been trying to help. It was Ian who was behaving badly.

But hearing Catherine talk about how comfortable she had been during her time with Dr. Parker made Laura feel pleased and, in an odd way, somehow responsible for her friend's having found an agreeable rapport with a professional whom Laura respected wholeheartedly. Laura knew she herself had nothing to do with Dr. Parker entering Catherine's life. But listening to her friend go on about Janet's kindness and sympathetic ear, she was perfectly willing to turn things around and take credit for the fact that Michael—who, after all, was her husband—had turned the Bishops on to the doctor in the first place.

Laura smiled across at her friend. If only Catherine would give her credit.

Shortly after four, Laura stood up. "I really should be going. I've got a pupil coming at five. Little Tommy Wilcox. I call him Mr. Thumbs. He's been playing "Chopsticks" for three-and-a-half years now."

"I never even got that far," Catherine admitted. Her eyes had a sad, dark look. In a second, they brightened. "Come here. I want to show you the clowns."

Catherine led her friend down the hallway to her studio. She paused at the entrance and pointed to a half-dozen clown dolls that lounged on a shelf.

Laura's eyes were drawn elsewhere.

"My God, Catherine," she said, stifling a gasp. "Did you do that one?"

Catherine followed her friend's eyes to the malevolent doll who seemed to be staring through Laura Spinoza.

"Yes, Laura. Isn't he beautiful?"

Laura moved closer to the doll, inspecting it curiously. Catherine leaned against the wall, taking in the tableau with satisfaction.

"Do you want the truth?" Laura asked finally. "He kind of gives me the creeps."

Catherine's hands went to her throat. A mischievous grin had crossed her face. Her fingers closed around the doll-figure necklace Laura had given her.

Catherine removed the necklace and placed it around the neck of the malevolent child doll. "There. Doesn't it look better on him?"

Involuntarily, Laura drew back. For the merest glimpse of an instant, the tiny figurines on the necklace appeared to tremble in fear at their proximity to an evil as ancient as time itself.

Chapter Nine

"Catherine?"

Ian stood in the doorway of the apartment. Hearing no response to his announcement that he was home from work, he ventured inside. His milky eyes wandering around the room, he took off his jacket and tossed it roughly on the couch.

Mrs. Roberts entered from the kitchen, her slippered feet padding noiselessly. "Mr. Bishop?"

Ian whirled around guiltily, as if he didn't belong in his own apartment. He scowled at the old woman. "Where's my wife?"

The housekeeper stared him down. "She's taking a nap. Dinner will be ready in an hour."

Ian strode to the bar and looked for the workings of a martini. He sensed Mrs. Roberts hesitating in the doorway.

"Yes," he said, without turning around. Ian prided himself on his intuition, once he knew something was in the vicinity.

"Mr. Bishop," the housekeeper said forcefully, though with a plaintive dark tone. "Do you think perhaps I could have a word with you?"

Ian opened a bottle of gin. "Of course, Mrs. Roberts. What is it?"

The housekeeper hesitated. "I don't want to keep you from your cocktail."

"Nonsense," Ian replied magnanimously. "A drink can always wait. What's on your mind?"

Mrs. Roberts glanced around. When she finally spoke, her voice was slightly more than a whisper.

"Well, this morning I was going down the hall. I was bringing some towels to the linen closet. I heard Mrs. Bishop's voice. She was having a conversation with someone. I thought she was on the telephone. But I happened to glance into the studio. And she was all alone. She was talking to someone that wasn't there. Someone named Bobo."

Ian's face blanched with undisguised displeasure. His voice sounded tightly unconcerned. "You know how Mrs. Bishop can be. Sometimes she treats those dolls as if they're real."

"Pardon me, Mr. Bishop, but I don't think she was talking to one of the dolls."

"What are you saying?"

The housekeeper lowered her eyes. Her voice grew even softer. "I don't know. She just didn't seem like herself."

"Meaning what?" Ian asked, losing the struggle to control his annoyance.

"I do hope she's all right," the old woman said more firmly. "I know she's been seeing a doctor."

Ian's voice rose as he said, "She's been seeing a psychologist."

"Yes, of course, I meant that—"

"And she's perfectly all right!"

Ian glared at Mrs. Roberts, then spun on his heel and charged toward the bedroom. The housekeeper followed his movements with an air of superiority.

Ian opened the bedroom door noisily, but Catherine did not stir. She was asleep on top of the covers, her body curled up into a question mark.

Ian shook her abruptly. Catherine whirled out of her sleep and sat up in bed, startled.

"Oh, you frightened me!"

Ian loomed over his wife. His shadow bobbed on the wall like a dark, elongated figure from a 1920s expressionist horror movie.

"I'll do more than frighten you if I don't get an explanation."

Catherine rubbed sleep out of her gorgeous eyes. She looked like a little girl.

"Ian, what's wrong?"

"You tell me," Ian barked. "I come home from work and my housekeeper tells me that my wife is wandering around talking to herself like a fucking lunatic!"

"I wasn't talking to myself."

"Great! You were talking to Bobo! That makes it all right. I don't like it, Catherine. I don't like you pretending that this character Bobo really exists. You know better."

Tears were inching down Catherine's face. She brushed them away with her fingers. "I can't help it."

"You'd better start to help it. I'll be goddamned if I'm going to sit around listening to you talking to God knows what. What is he? A gnome? A leprechaun? How come nobody else can see him? Is he here now? Bobo, are you there? Maybe he's under the bed, huh?"

"Ian, please, he'll get angry."

"He'll get angry! I don't believe this!"

Ian was pounding one meaty fist into the palm of his other hand. He looked animallike. Suddenly, he stopped. He studied his wife for a moment. Catherine's sobbing subsided.

"Catherine?"

"Could you hand me a tissue?"

"Why don't you ask Bobo?" Ian exploded. "Let Bobo hand you a tissue."

Ian reached across to the night table. He tugged a tissue from its container, then gave it to his wife. He put a hand authoritatively on her shoulder, which trembled to his touch. He spoke in a voice that seemed poised between anger and some form of recital.

"Catherine, I'm going to say something and I want you to listen. Bobo does not exist. He's not real. I don't want you talking to him. I want you to stop this nonsense. I want you to be the girl that I married. If something's wrong, I want you to talk to me. I'm your husband. I don't want you calling on some nonexistent person."

Catherine looked up at her husband. Her eyes glimmered. "I haven't, Ian. Bobo calls on me."

Chapter Ten

"Tell me about Bobo."

Catherine sat in her customary place in Janet Parker's office. The doctor had a steno pad opened on her lap.

Catherine sighed. Her eyes went around the room once before she began. "Well, I haven't thought about him since I was eight years old, but he seems to be back in my life."

"He was your imaginary playmate?"

Catherine hesitated. "To me, he's very real."

"He went away after your father's injury?"

"I think so. Yes."

"Why do you think he's come back?"

"I don't know," Catherine admitted, her voice a melodic whisper in the muted room. "He hasn't told me."

Animus

Janet made a few notes on her pad. She let a minute go by before she spoke. "Did you ever hear the word Animus?"

"Animus?" Catherine paused. "No."

"In Jungian psychology, Animus is the inner force that exists in each person. In a woman, it's Animus, the masculine aspect of her being. In a man, it's Anima, the feminine aspect of his being. Your Animus, for example, represents the classic male traits: strength, courage, the hunter instinct. A man's Anima represents the classic female traits: intuition, compassion, the emotions."

Catherine turned slightly. She looked puzzled. "What's all that got to do with Bobo?"

Janet hesitated. "Well, in a sense, Bobo might be your Animus—your masculine drive—trying to communicate with you. As a child, a person's Animus often takes form as an imaginary playmate. All children have imaginary playmates."

Catherine giggled. "I can't believe that Ian had an imaginary playmate."

"No?"

Catherine resumed her serious look. "He says he never did," she answered quietly.

"Of course he did. He just doesn't remember. Most of us can't recall them once we mature."

All at once, Catherine looked hopeful in a childlike way. "Did you have one?" she asked.

Janet nodded cheerfully. "Sure. His name was Wally. We were great friends. He used to protect me, just like Bobo protects you."

"Why do I need protection? Now, I mean."

"Well, something in your life, some recent events—you might be feeling threatened."

Catherine's eyes wandered away. "I can't think of anything. I don't feel threatened."

"We're speaking about the subconscious," Janet reminded her. "You may not be aware of what you're feeling."

A moment went by. Catherine gave no response.

"Let's get back to the dream," the psychologist suggested. "In the dream, you're feeling unloved. You're vulnerable. You want your father's approval and he doesn't give it to you. So what happens?"

More silence. Catherine's body had stiffened.

"Bobo consoles you," Janet continued. "Bobo comes to your rescue."

"What are you saying?"

"As a child, when you felt unloved, even threatened, you sought out Bobo, your Animus. Now, as an adult, you may be doing the same thing subconsciously. You think Bobo is seeking you out, but it's the other way around."

"I don't feel unloved," Catherine said, a touch of defensiveness in her voice. "My father was cold to me. That's true. But Ian loves me. He takes good care of me."

"Do you see any similarities between Ian and your father?"

"I was waiting for that," Catherine replied sarcastically. "I married my father figure, is that it?"

Dr. Parker gave her patient a kindly smile. "It's a possibility. Women are often attracted to men who remind them of their father."

"Not this woman," Catherine said quietly. "I was afraid of my father. I'm not afraid of Ian."

"Are you sure?"

Chapter Eleven

The Evil danced crazily from one barren place to another. It blew on the Earth and caused floods. It shot out of hot lava. It spit its cold breath on the land and there was ice. It watched in delight as living matter formed into a more complicated species. And as man stood upright, the Evil hovered just out of eyesight. It became what man feared.

Wednesday night. Seven o'clock.

Outside the Bishop Gallery, a thin young man paced the sidewalk, puffing feverishly on a menthol cigarette.

Andrew Garron, a Cincinnati artist in New York for his first showing, was nervous. He was one of the three painters being introduced tonight under the ironic collective title of *Three Primitives*.

Andrew ran a pallid hand across the top of his crew-cut head. He could feel the sweat coming off his scalp. It was only the second time Andrew had been in New York. The first was in 1979 when he had almost been arrested for grand larceny. That was before he had become a real painter, and he'd been staying at the YMCA on West 63rd Street. Some trouble about another guest's missing jewelry. Andrew had been questioned by the police, but there was nothing to hold him on. The watch and bracelets were safe in a locker at the Port Authority Bus Terminal.

Andrew was only 21, but he had lived a good deal in his short span on earth. The son of divorced parents, he'd been raised in Louisville, but crossed the river to Cincinnati when his mother got custody of him and his sister Alice. By the age of 15, Andrew had been in and out of public schools and picked up a liking for art and a facility at painting that promised a ticket to greener pastures. Dreading the last two years of high school and even the thought of college, he'd shipped off on a freighter for the Gulf of Mexico and lived for a time in the French Quarter of New Orleans and, later, in the back streets of Caracas. He supported himself with the odd painting and a steadily burgeoning career as a drug runner working out of the Florida Keys. By the time he was 20, he'd been around the world twice, had dined with a few princes and barons and was ready to devote himself to a full-time dedication to art, which he pursued with only the occasional detour toward swindling and smuggling.

Andrew knew he was an interesting—and, more importantly, a very savvy and commercial—painter. So when he'd sent away his slides to Ian Bishop in New York (at the recommendation of a 70-year-old art lover with a taste for brown heroin), he hadn't been that surprised to receive an invitation to exhibit.

Andrew lit a new cigarette off the old one and took a lung-ravaging puff. Now he was one of three primitives. The name of the exhibition pleased him. He was primitive all right, but it was a savage world. He was even more pleased that his two fellow primitives would not be there tonight. One, an Italian named Pandolfo, had been detained at U.S. Customs on suspicion of terrorist activities. The other, an eccentric Hopi Indian from Taos, New Mexico, was too sick, or too primitive, to travel.

Despite his elation, Andrew was sweating at the thought of what lay ahead. Andrew didn't like social gatherings and, given what had happened during his previous visit to New York, he never knew who would turn up. Maybe that police inspector who had questioned him in that small, dimly lit room on 63rd Street and never believed his story. That night in 1979,

Andrew believed that it was possible for one man to stare into the heart of another and penetrate to the darkest and most hidden recesses of his private thoughts.

Andrew reached in the pocket of his blue pinstriped jacket. He took out a black bandanna, folded it and wrapped it tightly over his head. He smiled grimly at his reflection in the glass of the gallery entrance. No sweat. Hanging on the door was a metal sign: *Closed For Private Reception.*

Inside the gallery, everything was in readiness for the opening night party. A buffet had been laid out. Waiters and bartenders had arrived. Champagne was on ice. All the paintings had been hung and checked with measuring devices for perfect alignment. Ian always insisted on that.

Standing by her desk, Lisa Gamble, dressed in a stylish gray pants suit topped with an ivory necklace, was talking to Ian on the phone.

"Everything's fine," she reported. "Your limousine is on the way."

"Melissa?" There was a breath of eagerness in Ian's voice on the line.

"She should be there in five minutes."

"Perfection."

"Wait till you see the food. There's enough pâté here to feed Rhode Island."

"Are you saying we ordered too much?" Ian asked quickly.

"No, but there's plenty. What we don't eat, we can always put out for the homeless."

Ian responded with a dry chuckle. "For heaven's sake, why should we waste it?"

"I beg your pardon."

"What did the homeless ever do for us?"

In the bedroom of the Bishop apartment, Ian put down the receiver. He was sitting on the bed, dressed in a tuxedo minus the jacket, which hung on a nearby table. Across the room, Catherine was at her dressing table, applying makeup. She was nearly dressed. She put away her lipstick and went into the adjoining bathroom. A second later, Ian heard the water running.

Ian got into his tuxedo jacket. He inspected his tie in the bedroom mirror. Suddenly, he heard a voice from the bathroom. It was Catherine's voice, low but still audible. She sounded hollow.

"Shhh. Not now, Bobo. I can't talk to you now."

Ian turned from the mirror. He went stealthily toward the bathroom. He stood by the half-open door, watching Catherine, who couldn't see him.

Catherine was staring at the tile squares on the bathroom wall. Her lovely hazel eyes were round and vacant.

"Yes, I am a little nervous. Do I look all right?"

Animus

A pause, as though for a reply. Catherine giggled.

"I don't feel like a princess."

Another pause. Someone—*something*—was speaking to Catherine from inside the white-squared bathroom wall.

Catherine smiled shyly.

"Thank you, Bobo."

Ian stepped into the brightness of the room. Catherine spied him in the mirror. She looked embarrassed.

Ian opened his mouth to speak, but Catherine put her long, exquisite fingers over his mouth. She looked at him almost pleadingly.

"I know Bobo's not here in the room," she whispered, "but he's in here."

Catherine put her hand over her heart.

Chapter Twelve

Two hours later.

The opening of *Three Primitives* was in full swing. More than 200 people were in attendance, availing themselves determinedly of the buffet and the open bar, with occasional dutiful glances at the works of art that had, theoretically at least, occasioned the evening.

Soft classical music played discreetly in the background, a sonata by Mozart. Several society page columnists—Ian always courted them shamelessly—and a dozen or more art critics were present, the less self-conscious of them, from time to time, jotting down notes or speaking their observations on the event into mini-tape recorders.

Lisa Gamble was the perfect hostess, moving

adroitly through the crowd, introducing guests
to one another and pointing out the artworks.
Ian was in a corner of the room, opposite the
door, taking a position from which he could
observe everything going on in the gallery. At
intervals, he would glide out from his self-
imposed station, making quick forays into the
mob to accomplish some intricate goal; then,
just as suddenly, he would be back at his corner
post. Ian was in his element. His stance and
attitude telegraphed one persistent message: he
was in control.

Beside him, Catherine looked serene and
ethereal. Only the slight trembling of her
delicate hands betrayed some inner feeling
of disorder. Once in a while, her left eye gave
a quick, anxious flicker.

In the opposite corner, Dr. Janet Parker
watched. Dressed in a form-fitting floral print
summer dress, she coolly sipped a bourbon and
water.

Even from across the room, through an end-
lessly swirling crowd of people, she could see
that Catherine Bishop was anxious. Janet had
had only a few words of greeting with her
patient earlier in the evening, and Catherine,
hanging on Ian's arm, had looked at her doubtfully, as though regretting the invitation she
had sent her the day before. Small wonder,
Janet thought. The girl was probably scared
to death.

Scared of what? Janet wondered. Certainly,

Ian had something to do with it. The way Catherine glanced at her husband nervously during the introduction betrayed a genuine fear of how he might react. But Ian had been cordial. A bit aloof, but polite. Still, there was an air of superiority about him, an unmistakable aura of dominance, as if, by signing the checks for Catherine's treatment, he was somehow in possession of Janet's wherewithal. As if he could regulate her by influencing her income. Janet had seen that type of behavior before. It was almost a given in her profession whether coming from patients or their guardians.

What a strange word. Guardian. Ian reminded Janet of some fierce, overbearing lord in a nineteenth-century English novel. Something the Brontes might have fashioned.

What did that make Catherine? the psychologist mused, taking another drink of bourbon. More a ward than a wife. More a helpless child than a spouse.

Easy, Janet, she cautioned herself. Maybe she was overreacting. But the way Ian's glance went guardedly toward Catherine and the way the young woman responded made her think she was not mistaken.

Catherine was fearful, she decided. But maybe not of Ian. All at once, Janet was certain that Catherine was afraid of someone else—*afraid of Catherine.*

Janet drifted across the room to within earshot of the couple. Ian was showing off a painting to Michael and Laura Spinoza, whom Janet had greeted earlier.

"See how the light brings out the texture of the orange?" Ian asked, his voice like that of an imperious professor. "If the painting were hung two inches lower, that would almost look red."

"Couldn't you adjust the track lights?" Michael wanted to know.

Ian sighed. He pointed to another painting. "Ah, but what would that do to Andrew's *Le Veilleur de Nuit*?"

Laura smiled. *"The Night Watchman* would look like he was on the day shift."

Ian laughed. "Exactly."

As she listened to the others, Janet watched Lisa Gamble negotiate her way through the crowd, amid the popping of flashbulbs. The psychologist had been welcomed by her at the door and found her cold and suspicious. In tow Lisa had a sickly looking man with a black bandanna over his head; Janet considered him positively frightening.

Lisa steered Andrew toward Ian and the others. The artist flashed a tight, yellow-toothed grin and, for the briefest of moments, reminded Janet Parker of a vampire.

"This is Andrew Garron," Ian said expansively. "One of my proteges. Next year, when I open my new gallery, my larger gallery, I intend to give him an entire show. Meet Michael and Laura Spinoza. Michael is my best friend."

Andrew nodded uncomfortably at the couple. Ian moved Catherine slightly forward as if she were on display. "My wife."

Andrew offered Catherine his hand. "*Enchanté,*" came absurdly from his lips.

"He just did a wonderful interview with Davis," Lisa Gamble announced. "I think we've got the cover of *Taste.*"

"Good," Ian noted. "Make sure you follow up on it first thing in the morning."

"There's the *Times,*" Lisa said dramatically. "We'll see you later."

Andrew smiled helplessly as he was dragged off by Lisa. More flashbulbs went off. With each shock of light, the artist shielded his eyes. Catherine, too, seemed to wince with every explosion. Watching from nearby, Janet made note of her reaction.

"Lisa seems efficient," Michael remarked.

Ian nodded. "Yes, I think I got a good one there. She's fairly bright. Cute ass too."

Laura stole a quick look at her husband and rolled her eyes upward.

"Cute ass?" Laura said. "Ian, you've always had such a way with words."

Michael grinned. "Ian's a college graduate."

Ian's expression was one of mock surprise. "I can't help it if I admire a woman's finer points. Look at Catherine. The first time I saw her, I said she's a knockout. Don't blame me if I've got good taste. It's a curse but I have to live with it every single day of my life."

Animus

Just then, still on the outskirts of the group, Janet Parker happened to glance at Catherine Bishop. The younger woman seemed preoccupied, totally removed from the conversation. Her large hazel eyes were focused like headlights on something across the room. Her face was otherwise expressionless, her pretty mouth drawn down to reveal her teeth, which seemed to glisten with a feral intensity.

As though suspended on puppet string, Catherine went forward. She moved slowly but purposefully across the room. Her head was held high, her troubled hazel eyes riveted on her destination. Her arms rose up as though of their own power until they reached a horizontal level before her, giving her the appearance of a somnambulist.

The gallery sounds—the tinkling of glasses, the Mozart, the endless chatter—washed over Catherine's mind like ocean waves on some distant beach.

"Stunning exhibit," an elderly dowager observed, as the gallery sleepwalker glided by.

Catherine reached the wall. Her gaze was directed at a large somber canvas, the work of Andrew Garron. Black on darker black, it depicted the outline of a Death's Head against a nightmare of swirling horror. Below it was a small gold plaque with the title: *La Bête Intérieure*.

Catherine stared at the painting. She was strangely transfixed. In her head, the party noises had become oddly muted, as though they were being funneled to her through ominous, muffling clouds.

Seemingly helpless to control her own actions, Catherine reached up. She ran her hand slowly, almost questioningly, along the surface of the heavily textured painting.

Her fingers went to the Death's Head. Seconds went by. All sound had ceased in Catherine's brain, save for the rough, sensual rubbing of the painting's core of dread.

Catherine shifted her hands so that her long, bloodred fingernails were perpendicular to the canvas. She smiled benignly. She began to exert pressure with her nails, scraping off fragments of black paint from the Death's Head.

Suddenly, hands grasped her violently by the wrists. Roughly, Ian spun her away from the painting.

"What are you doing?" Ian demanded furiously, trying to keep from shouting.

His voice exploded into Catherine's consciousness. She blinked her eyes. Everyone in the gallery was watching, stock-still. There was not a sound.

Ian pulled her farther from the canvas. "You know never to touch a painting!"

Catherine looked up at him with wide, innocent eyes. She smiled beguilingly. "Bobo wanted to feel it."

Ian looked at her incredulously. His eyes

went darting around excitedly, his rage tempered only by his drive to preserve professional calm and dignity.

Across the room, he could see Dr. Parker taking in everything. Ian inhaled a deep breath. He put his arm protectively around Catherine and ushered her toward the front door of the gallery. The room was still hushed.

"Excuse us, please," Ian told the crowd, his voice even, almost casual. "My wife Catherine is not feeling well. It's nothing serious."

Once outside on the pavement, Ian dragged Catherine rudely toward the double-parked limousine. He shoved her into the back seat and got in beside her. Closing the door, he instructed Melissa to drive to the corner.

The car began moving. Ian closed the partition to cut off the driver. He turned angrily to Catherine, who looked confused and frightened.

"You made a fool of me in there," Ian hissed. "The most important opening of my fucking life and you tried to ruin it! You know who's in there? Only the leading art critics in the city, investors, the whole art community, my friends."

"Ian, I'm sorry," Catherine said. She was crying. Her voice sounded like soft rain.

"You're sorry! You're fucking sorry! What do you think those people are saying right now? What do you think they're saying?"

"I don't know."

"I'll tell you what they're saying. They're saying Ian Bishop has a wife who doesn't know the first thing about how to conduct herself in public! They're probably saying that Ian Bishop is married to a fucking imbecile!"

"I'm sorry."

"You know never to touch a painting! What's wrong with you, Catherine?"

"Ian, please. . . ."

"You dug your nails into that canvas. That painting is probably ruined. Everybody saw you do it. I'm going to have to go back there and face those people, try to salvage the rest of the evening. Ian Bishop is going to have to rescue tonight's opening from the disaster that you have perpetrated. That is not something Ian Bishop wants to do!"

"I want to go home," Catherine said meekly.

Ian slammed his fist against the cushion of the back seat. "You bet you're going home. You've done enough damage tonight. If you've got to run your claws over something, run them over those fucking dolls you've got!"

The limo had reached the corner. Ian jumped out and slammed the door.

Catherine sat in the back seat. She could hear her husband talking to the driver through the side window. "Take Mrs. Bishop home."

The driver nodded. The car sped off. Catherine turned to see Ian striding angrily toward his gallery.

Catherine's face was vacant. She could feel

the limousine cruising effortlessly uptown. For the first time, she noticed that the streets were slick with rain. It must have showered while she had been in the gallery enjoying the exhibition.

Catherine felt as though time had changed. She could have been at the reception for one hour, one day, even one year. She pressed against the corner of the back seat. More tears cascaded down her face. She was oblivious to the damp streets sliding by the window like moving platforms.

When she spoke aloud, Catherine's voice was in singsong. A high-pitched refrain of childlike innocence.

"Ian's mad. This time he's really mad. You shouldn't have done that, Bobo. You shouldn't have made me touch that painting. You're gonna get me in trouble. Why did you come back, Bobo?"

Catherine waited for a reply. The sleek black car rolled through the shining night streets, its wheels hissing below the floorboards.

Catherine waited. She cocked her head slightly, as though listening to someone. Suddenly, her eyes widened.

"I need you?" she asked, her voice husky and, at once, reassured.

Chapter Thirteen

Evelyn Roberts, the Bishops' housekeeper, was, as Catherine suspected, pushing 80 years of age. And as Catherine had noted, she had a spunkiness unusual for her years, due, no doubt, to a strict regimen of health food and exercise, which she had maintained for her entire life.

Born Evelyn Stephens in 1907 in the Earls Court section of London, she was the seventh and last child of working-class parents. Her father was a bricklayer who prided himself on providing food and shelter for his large family, but the going had never been easy. Evelyn remembered her childhood as a succession of catastrophes, generally involving the rent, and before she was ten, the Stephens clan had moved half a dozen times.

Still, her parents were cheerful sorts, and the children were brought up to believe that their lot was better than some, if not as good as most. When the Great War came, George Stephens put down his bricklayer's tools and joined the infantry. Two years later, he was dead, the victim of a German sniper.

Evelyn had to leave school and become a house servant, working for a family in Lancashire. Though she had once dreamed of being a dancer, Evelyn ended up working in a series of domestic household jobs—in London, in Surrey, and for a long spell in Edinburgh, before going to America and finding employment with a widower in Charleston, South Carolina. When he had succumbed to natural causes at the age of 91, Evelyn had ventured to New York, where she worked for ten years on Park Avenue before joining the Bishops shortly prior to their wedding.

Evelyn had been married briefly between the wars to a gambler named Nigel Roberts, who abandoned her after a few months for another woman. Later, Evelyn learned, he had been shot during a card game in Nice, while waiting on a yacht for another female companion. Evelyn never remarried—the experience had left her bitter and, she liked to think, wiser about human behavior. One could argue that it also speeded her way down a path familiar to students of English eccentricity.

*   *   *

The night of Ian's show, around 9:30, Mrs. Roberts was nearly ready for sleep. The apartment was quiet, just the way she liked things. The rain that evening had made her scowl with displeasure, forcing her to raise the volume on the radio next to her bed, which was broadcasting Bizet's *The Pearl Fishers*.

The housekeeper's room reflected her old-world British sensibilities. The single bed was covered with a hand-crocheted quilt that had been in her family for generations. On the two armchairs nearby were lace doilies going back to Earls Court. The mahogany dresser held an assortment of silver-framed photos from long ago. The windowsills were lined with plants, which Mrs. Roberts tended carefully, a skill she had learned as a little girl and never forgotten. The room was her little nest.

At the moment, Mrs. Roberts was propped up in bed reading a scandalous English newspaper. A lifelong devotee of the British Royal Family, she nonetheless felt an urgent need to monitor all reports of their activities, down to the most outlandish rumors, much as she disapproved of such yellow journalism as the kind she was reading with fascination that very evening.

Hearing sounds from the living room, she perked up. That was odd. Both Mr. Bishop and his wife were out for the evening. Mrs. Roberts glanced at the night table. Just 9:30.

Another noise.

Quickly, the housekeeper slid from beneath the covers. Her slippers were waiting for her at the foot of the bed. She tiptoed to the door. She opened it a crack.

Something flew past her on the way to the master bedroom.

Mrs. Roberts nodded her head knowingly. You could never be sure about the Bishops when they said they had plans for the night.

The old woman paused for a moment, then shut her door.

Under the covers. Where it was cool and safe. Lights off. But moonlight filled the room. Eyes closed. Restful. Calm.

Suddenly, Catherine's eyes shot open.

"Bobo?" she called out apprehensively.

No answer. Relax. No one in the room.

Wrong. Someone. Almost visible. Close enough to touch.

Abruptly, Catherine shuddered with a surprised sensuality.

"Bobo, don't. . . ."

Again. Oh. . . .

"Please, don't. . . ."

Catherine pushed back the bedcovers. She felt the cool air of the room along the contours of her nude body.

She licked her lips slightly. Gently, she ran her hands along her breasts, watching the nipples spring up hard to her touch.

Her touch?

Catherine smiled.

"Bobo," she moaned. "Yes. Oh, yes."

She was breathing heavily. Her body arched upward ever so slightly.

Her hands felt below her waist.

Her hands?

"Oh, that feels good. Don't stop. Oh, yes."

Catherine was moaning louder now. Her body rocked achingly on the bed.

Invisible lover.

Filled with ecstasy, Catherine cried out. "Oh, God, yes, yes!"

Catherine was thrown back violently against the headboard. A flood of warmth was overcoming her. Reassuring. Her eyes sparkled with fright and surprised abandon.

Just outside the closed door of the master bedroom, wrapped in a housecoat, stood an attentive Mrs. Roberts. Her ear was pressed to the door.

She had been eavesdropping on the sounds from the bedroom for quite some time. The look on Mrs. Roberts's face was a mixture of Victorian disapproval and unabashed curiosity.

"My, my," she muttered as she tiptoed in her slippered feet back to her room. "Those two are like animals."

Chapter Fourteen

Andrew Garron, looking weary and chalk faced, emerged from the Bishop Gallery. He breathed deeply of the wet night air. Immediately, his fingers went to his pocket for a crumpled pack of cigarettes. He lit up and inhaled ferociously. Goddamned no-smoking rules, he cursed, glancing back at the gallery. Pretty soon, he wouldn't be able to enjoy a cigarette in his own bathtub.

Andrew had been in a kind of daze for more than an hour. Ever since Catherine Bishop had gone to his painting and scraped her fingernails across it. She had defaced *La Bête Intérieure*. Andrew knew he should be angry. Outraged. But he was strangely excited.

It had to do with her eyes. . . .

She was a lovely woman, that Mrs. Bishop. Breathtaking. Andrew sucked on his cigarette. Even her name was beautiful.

"Catherine. . . ."

Andrew startled himself by saying the name aloud. People were milling around on the sidewalk. Others were leaving the gallery, saying good night to Ian and Lisa at the door.

Andrew hunched his shoulders. He drew back into the shadows, away from the exiting party guests.

Something about her eyes.

Andrew could still see her, approaching his canvas, walking like some mesmerized maiden in a vampire movie. So innocent. So helpless. Her eyes were like glittering jewels, shining on the painting that Andrew had loved more than any of his other creations.

Where had he seen a look like the one she had in her eyes? He'd encountered such a look before, but where?

Suddenly, a shiver ran through Andrew Garron. The police inspector who had interrogated him about the YMCA theft. He'd been able to look into Andrew and penetrate to his deepest core. His mind. His heart. Catherine had looked into *La Bête Intérieure* in the same way. She had penetrated to the Death's Head.

The heart of pure evil.

As Michael and Laura Spinoza came out of the Bishop Gallery, Ian took them aside. He looked weary.

"You go ahead," he instructed. "Take the limousine to Elaine's. I'll join you later on. I want to check on Catherine."

"What about Lisa?" Michael asked.

"She's going to clean up."

"I hope Catherine's okay," Laura offered.

Ian looked at her icily. "There's nothing wrong with Catherine. She's just tired."

Once the limousine was moving eastward, Laura turned to Michael.

"Nothing wrong with Catherine?" she asked sarcastically. "He practically hurled her out of the gallery."

Michael smiled thinly. "You said yourself Ian was a caveman. He's had a busy day. This morning, he discovered fire. After lunch, he started fooling around with the wheel."

"I'm serious. Catherine's been acting even stranger than usual. I told you what she did with that necklace I gave her. That doll she put it on was absolutely grotesque. Did you see the look on her face tonight when she was touching the painting?"

"What about it?"

"It was eerie—like she couldn't help herself. Like she was out of control."

Michael nodded. "Did you hear what she said? 'Bobo wanted to feel it.'"

"Yeah. What do you suppose that means? Who's Bobo?"

"I don't know. But I've got a feeling Ian is going to find out."

*   *   *

Mrs. Roberts was dozing, but the sound of the key in the apartment's front door brought her instantly awake. She looked at her bedside clock. It was after eleven.

The old woman went to her door. She opened it slightly. Seeing Ian, she was relieved. She opened her door farther.

Ian glanced her way. He frowned.

"You startled me," Mrs. Roberts said hoarsely. "I didn't hear you go out."

Ian twirled his key ring. "I beg your pardon."

Mrs. Roberts looked confused. "Well, when you and Mrs. Bishop came in before, I thought you had returned for the night."

"What are you talking about?" Ian asked impatiently.

"I didn't hear you go out."

"Mrs. Bishop returned by herself," Ian said, with the air of one speaking to a small child. "I, on the other hand, have been out all evening."

Mrs. Roberts put her hand to her throat. "Oh, I thought I heard you."

She nodded her head toward the master bedroom, but left the sentence hanging. She seemed confused and strangely frightened. Slowly, her face reddened with embarrassment.

Ian scarcely noticed her behavior. He was worn and exasperated. His formal clothes were wilting on his muscular frame.

Ian walked past Mrs. Roberts to his bedroom. The old woman retreated into her own room, looking thoroughly frightened.

Upon reaching the main bedroom, Ian could feel the anger he'd been harboring since the gallery incident start to dissipate.

Catherine's face on her pillow was bathed in the glow of moonlight. She was sleeping serenely.

Ian went closer. He was about to wake her, but just as his hand went to touch her neck, he thought better of it. He'd let her sleep. She looked so much like the Catherine of old, the shy, beautiful girl who had charmed him into her life.

Tenderly, Ian brushed a fold of his wife's chestnut hair back from her freckled face. He watched her for several moments, his expression a blend of concern and disapproval.

"My poor little girl," he said under his breath. "What am I going to do with you?"

"I don't want to hear about Animus, Catherine."

It was eight o'clock the following morning. The curtains of the Bishop bedroom were open and the room was bathed in morning sun. Ian and Catherine sat opposite each other at a glass-topped table on which sat two coffee cups. Confrontation was a palpable presence in the air-cooled chamber.

"Well, you're going to hear about Animus. It's

109

important. Dr. Parker thinks Animus might be what Bobo is all about."

"Bobo's all about your inability to deal with reality."

"Good, Ian. That's a nice simple explanation, neatly tied up in a package. Just the way you like it."

"Catherine, I've read Jung. I know about Animus. I don't see what it has to do with a figment of your imagination."

"Janet thinks Bobo could be my Animus, my masculine drive, trying to get in touch with me."

"And why would that be happening?"

"Because I'm feeling threatened."

"Bullshit."

"Because I need protection."

"Protection from what? I'm your husband. I'll protect you. That's my job."

"In my dream, I'm vulnerable. I'm afraid of my father. Bobo rescues me. He comforts me."

"And?"

"Now, in my life, I'm vulnerable again—so Bobo has reappeared."

"And the next thing you know, you're making an ass of yourself at my gallery."

"Do you want to listen to me or not?"

"I want you to make sense."

"I'm trying to explain to you why I touched the painting."

"Why you touched the painting? Why you

raked your nails across it? Why you ruined it in front of everybody?"

Catherine sighed. She stood up and went to the window. Outside, an already fiery sun was glistening off the windows of skyscrapers.

"That's what bothers you the most, Ian. 'In front of everybody.' "

"What bothers me the most is that you do something completely irrational and then try to tell me you were compelled to do it by your Animus. Your imaginary playmate."

"I'm just telling you what happened. If you don't want to believe me—"

"I don't want to believe you!" Ian shouted. "I don't want to hear any more about Bobo, about Animus, about your imaginary playmate."

Catherine spun around. She locked eyes with her husband.

"Okay, you don't want to hear it. You won't hear it."

The sun blazed off the glass-topped table that separated them. Head down, Catherine left the room.

Chapter Fifteen

The Evil was the substance of nightmares. It was the essence of terror before there was a word to describe that sensation. And when the Earth was young and there were only a few inhabiting it, there were those who worshiped the Evil, who opened their arms to that inviting darkness. And the Evil went inside those and saw the world through the humans' eyes. Felt with human hands. Killed with those same hands.

Hull College, which both Ian Bishop and Michael Spinoza had attended, was not an Ivy League institute of learning, but in its own way it was as academically desirable as Harvard or Yale. Tucked away in the northeastern part of Vermont, within shouting distance of

Dartmouth but nowhere near as famous, Hull was founded in 1867 by a former Union Army general who retired from the military to pursue his dream of founding a liberal arts college in a setting of green bucolic splendor.

Spread out over 50 acres, Hull had, from its inception, established itself as an elite college which catered to the upper class while making financial adjustments to admit poorer students. So it was that Ian, who came to Hull on an exchange program from an exclusive English school, was able to attend along with Michael, who won a scholarship that plucked him out of New York and what would have been a city college education. After spending his sophomore year at Hull, Ian was so taken with the school's peaceful country atmosphere and relaxed, free-thinking faculty that he tranferred there for his remaining college years.

On the Friday evening two nights after Ian's gallery opening, Hull College was very much on Ian's mind as he sat at the bar of Orion's, an Upper East Side pub not far from the Spinoza apartment. It was about six o'clock and the cheerful wood-dominated establishment was beginning to fill up, though it would be at least another hour before Orion's predominantly singles clientele would arrive from their downtown after-work bars.

Ian and Michael were at a corner of the bar, where they had an expansive view of the long, oak-paneled room and its beamed ceiling. In the back, past a couple of gigantic television screens broadcasting the local news, Orion's restaurant area was visible. Michael had a half-full mug of ale on the counter before him. Ian's cocktail glass was nearly empty.

In the midst of recounting an elaborate story, Ian let his voice boom out over the bar. "Then the dean held up this pair of panties and said, 'Mr. Spinoza, do you recognize these?' "

Beside him, Michael was sputtering with laughter into the remains of his drink.

"And you said: 'Yes, Dean, and you ought to recognize them too. They're your daughter's.' "

Ian's roar of laughter joined Michael's and the two men slapped each other playfully. Ian drained his cocktail and motioned to the bartender.

"Another vodka martini, sir?"

"Straight up, olive," Ian ordered.

The bartender turned to Michael. "You, sir?"

"No. I'm all right."

Ian leaned back on his barstool. "I wonder whatever happened to the dean's daughter. What was her name?"

Michael thought for a minute. "Charlotte?"

Ian bared his teeth in a smile. "Charlotte, indeed. She was a hot little number."

"Didn't you hear?"

"Hear what, Michael?"

"She married Howie Blume. They're operating a trailer park in Alabama."

Ian ducked his head comically. "Jeez."

"Don't laugh. He might have driven up here in one of his trailers. He might be at tonight's reunion."

Both men laughed. The bartender returned with Ian's vodka martini.

"Maybe we ought to get something to eat," Michael suggested.

The bartender lingered expectantly. Ian studied his glass a bit morosely.

"You think we should eat?" Ian asked Michael.

"Well, there's going to be a lot of drinking at the reunion. It's not good to drink on an empty stomach."

Ian shrugged. "We'll eat when we get there. Here, have a peanut."

Ian pushed a peanut dish along the bar toward Michael. With his other hand, he dismissed the bartender.

"Remember Richie Bendix?" Ian asked loudly. "He used to sleepwalk on the football field?"

Michael smiled grimly. "Our whole varsity used to sleepwalk on the football field."

Ian guffawed. The two men slapped each other on the back. Michael ordered another glass of ale.

An hour later, Ian and Michael emerged from the pub. Ian was decidedly unsteady on his feet.

Michael glanced at the western sky visible at the end of the crosstown street. Later, he would remember that the sky was unusually red that night, as if the sun were setting in a pool of blood.

"Which way?" Ian asked jovially.

Michael pointed down the street. "It's just three blocks. We can walk it." He took another look at his companion. "*I* can walk it."

"What's that supposed to mean?" Ian asked. There was anger lurking just below his simple question.

"You okay?"

Ian steadied himself. He took a gulp of sultry night air.

"Never felt better in my life. Let's go."

They started down the street. Before they had reached the corner, Ian stopped.

"I should call Janet Parker."

Michael looked surprised. "Now? What for?"

Ian leaned against a lamppost. "I'm a bit pissed off at her. She's got Catherine spouting all kinds of Jungian psychology to me. I send my wife to a shrink because she's having bad dreams, and I get back Jung's theory of Animus. What a load of bullshit. And you're the one who recommended her."

"Ian, she's one of the top people in her field." Michael laughed. "She's even been on *Good Morning, America*."

"Well, I'm shelling out a hundred and fifty bucks an hour. She'd better get Catherine straight pretty quick."

In the western sky, the bloodred sun seemed to shimmer in anticipation.

Chapter Sixteen

Marburg Haus was on East 84th Street, a few doors off Third Avenue. Only a few blocks from Bavarian Castle and Rhine Vista, two of the more popular German restaurants in the Yorkville area, Marburg Haus, though less touristy, still laid claim to being one of the more popular and venerable eating establishments in the area. First opened in 1910, it had weathered two world wars in which Germany had been the enemy and, by catering slyly to both the German immigrant inhabitants of Yorkville and their non-German neighbors, it had become something of a Manhattan institution.

The front room of Marburg Haus was a spacious area in which the gemutlich atmosphere of rural Germany was encouraged. An oom-pah-pah band, comprised of ten men in lederhosen, saw to that. Nightly, the Essen & Fressen, as it was called, was filled with diners and beer drinkers, swaying to the familiar music and being served by thick-armed waitresses, many of whom had come over from Germany.

Behind the Essen & Fressen was the restaurant's Club Room, used for private functions. Snug, with a lower ceiling, it had been the site of Hull College reunions for as long as any of the alumni could remember.

One side of the room featured a private bar. Across from it was a long buffet table with a lavish assortment of German delicacies. Several large beer kegs were also set up on a table. A waiter clad in traditional Bavarian clothing stood ready to pour out pitchers of beer as they were needed. On that night, they were needed at quite regular intervals.

Ian and Michael stood near the bar, talking to several of their classmates. The room was rapidly filling up with alumni, many of whom were greeting old friends with enthusiasm.

Michael was sipping a beer, while Ian had already graduated to his second Marburg Haus martini.

"Did you see who just came in?" Michael asked.

He pointed over to the door, where a short, bearded man was hanging up his coat.

"Danny Van Doren," Ian said, his voice louder than was necessary to be heard above the room's occupants.

"Little Danny," Michael confirmed.

Ian stirred his drink. "Looks like he may have grown a few inches."

"Yeah, he's up to five two now."

A waiter came by with a tray of hors d'oeuvres. Michael pointed him out to Ian.

"Have some of that liverwurst."

"No, I'm not hungry."

"You haven't eaten anything."

Ian held up his martini glass. He scooped out the olive. "I've had five olives."

As Ian was leaning over the bar, trying to get the bartender's attention, the diminutive Danny Van Doren wandered over to join the group.

"How are you, Danny?" Michael greeted him.

"Just dandy," Van Doren replied. He carried a large mug of beer. When Ian turned back from the bar, he thrust out his hand toward the bigger man.

"Ian. I saw your picture in the paper. I didn't know you were pals with Andy Warhol."

Ian looked down at Danny disdainfully. "How's the appliance repair business?"

"I got fourteen people working for me, so I guess it must be all right."

Ian put his arm around Danny. "I haven't seen Danny in fifteen years. When we left off, he was heaving his guts out on the floor of the

Killarney Rose Tavern up on Webster Avenue in the Bronx. It was the best drinking contest I ever won. How much did I take you for that night?"

"I don't remember," Danny muttered.

"Fifty dollars? It was fifty dollars. I remember because I used that money to take Suzie Preston out to dinner. Remember Suzie Preston, Danny?"

"Sure. Everyone remembers Suzie."

"Didn't you used to have a crush on her?"

Seeing Danny Van Doren's discomfort, Michael moved to defuse what he knew could become a volatile situation.

"Hey, come on," he said with a wink toward Ian. "This is a party."

Ian ignored his friend. "Good old Suzie. Such a gorgeous young lady. And, I might add, a terrific piece of ass. She came across on the first date."

Danny Van Doren glared at Ian angrily. "So? Big fucking deal. I screwed her too."

Ian chuckled. He put a hand on Danny's shoulder. "I know. She told me all about it."

"What's that supposed to mean?"

"I'm not sure you want to pursue that subject, Danny."

Danny removed Ian's hand from his shoulder. "I asked you a question."

"Well, if you must know, Suzie Preston discussed your . . . how shall I put it? Your shortcomings."

Danny laughed a bit too loudly. "Get the fuck out of here. I don't think you even got near her."

"You're a short man, Danny," Ian said with mock politeness. "One can't expect you to have anything but small appliances."

"No lady has ever complained," Danny boasted.

"I know, Danny. We've all heard the old saying. It's not the meat, it's the motion."

"You better believe it."

"I'm afraid that's just an old wives' tale, Danny. Started by some old wife with a short husband—someone like you with a small dick."

Danny studied his taller antagonist for a moment. The crowd at the bar had grown during the exchange. Danny looked around. He chuckled. "What would you say to a rematch?"

Ian grinned. "Are you serious?"

"I'm dead serious. You beat me once in a drinking match, but I don't think you can do it again. In fact, five hundred dollars says you can't."

"That's a lot of money, Danny. Are you sure you can afford it on your wages?"

"Maybe I don't run an art store like you, but I do all right."

Ian raised an eyebrow. "Oh, I'm certain you do. Television sets are always breaking down."

"I do okay with VCRs too, believe me. So what do you say? Think you can beat me in a rematch, you putz?"

"*Putz*. Under the circumstances, I find that choice of word almost priceless. And in answer to your question, you're on. I hope you've learned how to hold your liquor."

Danny's face was a mixture of delight and bravado. "You'd be surprised."

Chapter Seventeen

A short time later, Ian and Danny sat across from each other at a circular table in the center of the back room. Each man had taken off his jacket, loosened his tie and rolled up his sleeves. The other alumni formed a circle around them. There was an air of expectancy in the room.

On the table were several large pitchers of beer and two shot glasses. Jim Neville, a burly red-haired man, assumed a referee's stance. Jim had been chosen for that assignment because he was judged to be equally friendly with Ian and Danny, the truth being that he hardly knew either man.

Jim rapped a knife against the side of a beer pitcher. The room quieted down. At Ian's side,

123

Michael Spinoza felt an odd sensation of doom.

"Okay," Jim hollered, trying to sound authoritative. "The rules are as follows. Each man is to drink a shot glass full of beer every thirty seconds. First man to give up or pass out is the loser. No vomiting. Belching is permitted. The bet is for five hundred dollars. Shake hands and come out drinking and ready to kick ass!"

Ian and Danny shook hands. The smaller man scowled at his adversary through narrow slits of eyes. Watching from beside Ian, Michael had the feeling Danny Van Doren wanted to settle a lifetime of debts that night. The little man's anger seemed directed at more than Ian and the memory of Suzie Preston. No, Danny was aiming higher than that, Michael guessed. Or lower. Hoping to erase many years of doubt, insecurity and the condescension only a small man may receive from the bullies of the world.

Michael sipped his Scotch. He had switched over to the harder stuff the minute the duel had begun to seem inevitable. Scotch put a harder edge on things, Michael knew. Though it was stronger, if he kept his intake down to two glasses, he'd be able to deal with the outcome of Ian's drinking contest with a clear head. It made no sense, Michael knew, but it had worked in the past. Something told him Michael would need to be alert and precise tonight, if only for Ian's well-being.

"Go!" Jim shouted.

Ian and Danny each threw back a shot glass full of beer. They put the glasses back on the table and Jim filled them up again. The battle had begun.

Ten minutes later. A large piece of cardboard, serving as a tote board, indicated that 20 shot glasses had been consumed by each man. Neither of the combatants seemed any the worse for wear.

Michael stood behind Ian, watching the contest carefully. Next to Michael stood Charlie, a tall ex-classmate Ian and Michael had known from the school rugby team. Jim poured out two more shot glasses.

"Number twenty-one," the referee announced.

Both contestants drained their glasses.

"I like Ian—for ten bucks," Charlie confided to Michael, whose eyes never left the playing field of the table, its cloth already soaked with spilled beer.

Michael was aware of a hubbub of voices. The circle of observers was growing more animated. Money was waved. Bets were agreed on. The duel was taking on the aura of a cockfight, Michael thought grimly.

He looked down at the back of Ian's neck. It was turning red. The hair that was curled there was already drenched in perspiration. Michael wished he were anywhere but there. He regretted ever having spoken to Ian about a school reunion. But it was too late.

Time passed. The drinking match continued. For Michael, it was as though he were seeing and hearing underwater. The room felt foreign.

Both Ian and Danny were sweaty and drunk. The betting of the onlookers continued. Their comments as they egged the contestants on grew louder and more frenzied.

Jim remained calm, continuing to fill up the glasses, consulting the stopwatch and toting the number of shots consumed. Waiters brought more pitchers of beer, their eyes betraying interest and disapproval at the same time.

Michael kept a close eye on Ian's condition. Had only 25 minutes gone by? The number on the tote board was approaching fifty.

Twenty minutes later, Ian and Danny had reached the level of being ridiculously inebriated. They were bleary eyed. Their faces were puffed and ruddy. Sweat poured from their foreheads. Their shirts were drenched. Their motions were sluggish.

They continued drinking.

A strange silence had settled on the proceedings. Michael felt as if he were witnessing some contest from a long-ago past. Some battle that had already been fought and won. Some mythic duel worthy of the gods.

Jim poured each man still another shot.

"Number ninety-two," he intoned gravely.

Ian drank his shot right down. Danny just stared at his glass in a stupor.

Michael leaned over to Ian. He could hear his friend's breath coming in rumbled fits and starts.

"You all right?" Michael asked him.

Ian turned to him. His eyes were rolling wildly in his head. His words, when they finally emerged from his beer-coated mouth, were thick and slurred.

"Piece of cake."

Across the table, Danny reached for his shot glass. Just before his fingers could encircle it, something unexpected interfered.

Danny collapsed on the table.

A cheer went up from the observers. Jim held up Ian's arm in a gesture of triumph.

"The winner and still champion."

Ian smiled crazily. Michael was worried. His friend was out of control.

When Michael and Ian finally emerged from Marburg Haus, Ian was still smarting from what he considered to be Danny Van Doren's bad sportsmanship. Not only had the smaller man refused to acknowledge Ian as a better beer drinker, but he had backed off from giving the victor cash (which Ian pointed out could easily be obtained from a nearby bank machine) in favor of sending him a check sometime next week (when he could transfer some money from another account, or so Danny claimed).

Ian was still livid about these matters as Michael tried walking him around, hoping to sober him up. Michael himself was a little drunk, but nothing compared to his friend. Ian was almost catatonic.

The pair of them made for an interesting sight as they walked in a rapidly larger circle at the corner of Third Avenue and East 84th Street. Both men were disheveled. Ian had lost his tie and somehow managed to tear his jacket.

"Out of my way!" Ian exclaimed as he swung drunkenly at a parking meter.

"Hey," Michael cautioned. "Take it easy. You're gonna break your hand."

"Fuck it."

Michael steered Ian over toward the doorway of a drugstore, where he would be less dangerous to those passing along on the sidewalk.

"I've never seen you like this, Ian. What the fuck's got into you?"

Ian thrust out his chest in imitation of Robert De Niro in *Taxi Driver*. "You talking to me?"

"What did you get so smashed for?"

"You talking to me?"

"Are you nuts or something?"

Ian grabbed Michael roughly by the collar. Spittle ran from his mouth onto his chin as he snarled out a slurred reply.

"I can tell you this, Michael, because you're my best friend. I never screwed Suzie Preston. She wouldn't let me!"

Ian giggled.

It was nearly eleven o'clock when a taxi pulled up outside the door of Ian's building. The doorman hurried out to open the car door.

Ian got clumsily out of the cab. Michael, on the seat beside him, looked concerned.

"Good evening, Mr. Bishop," the doorman said, pretending not to notice Ian's desperate condition.

Michael leaned out of the back seat. "Could you see him to the elevator?"

"Certainly, sir," the doorman said helpfully. Ian had given him a generous Christmas bonus and never forgot his birthday or, for that matter, those of his wife and children.

"I can see myself, thank you," Ian said woozily in what he thought was a W. C. Fields impression.

Ian pushed the doorman aside and staggered across the sidewalk toward the door of the building. He narrowly missed colliding with an elderly woman, who was walking with her dog, an old toddling poodle.

Michael and the doorman watched as Ian disappeared into the lobby.

"I'll see that he gets upstairs," the doorman offered.

Ed Kelleher & Harriette Vidal

Michael handed the man a bill. "I've never seen him this way before."

Later, in the cab going home to Laura, Michael wondered at the Western sky. It still held vicious streaks of bloodred slashes. The night air seemed to throb with an ancient, inexplicable presence.

Something evil stood ready to be unleashed.

Chapter Eighteen

When the time was right, the Evil discovered fire. And man became curious. With discovery came territory. With that came greed. And the detestable force grew even mightier. It was in the eye of a hurricane, the mad dance of a tornado, the relentless slashing of a tidal wave, the devastation of an earthquake. But that wasn't the worst of it.

Catherine was curled up on the sofa in the living room reading a book when she heard something outside. She drew the men's flannel robe that she was wearing more tightly around her. She put down her novel.

The knob of the front door was turning. There was the clatter of keys from the hallway.

Catherine looked up expectantly. The door to the apartment opened to reveal Ian, wavering dangerously. Catherine registered a look of surprise. Then she began to giggle.

"Look at Mr. Control," she said teasingly, as she got up to cross the room. "Must have been some party."

Ian threw the cluster of keys across the living room, narrowly missing a vase.

"Whoa, good shot, Ian," Catherine said, drawing up short. "I thought you liked that vase."

Ian started to take off his jacket. "What vase? I've never seen that vase before in my life."

Catherine helped him out of the coat. "Here, sit down. I'll fix you some coffee."

"Don't need coffee. Fix me a drink."

Catherine guided her husband toward the sofa. Ian slumped down, knocking her book to the floor.

"I think you've had enough to drink," Catherine said, trying not to sound harsh or reprimanding.

"Oh, you do, do you?"

"God, Ian, you smell like a brewery."

"I will have. . . ." Ian paused as if pondering a menu in an elegant restaurant. "I believe I will have a vodka martini. Straight up. Olive."

Catherine made no move to serve him. "College graduates, huh? I thought you guys were supposed to be bright."

"In a thin-stemmed glass, if you would be so kind."

"Is that what you did in school? Drank yourself stupid? It's a wonder you graduated."

"Where's my drink?"

"So this is it, huh?" Catherine's voice had taken on a drier tone. "Boys' night out?"

"Boys will be boys," Ian said gravely. He smiled at his own wit.

Catherine moved a hassock closer to the sofa. "Here. At least, put your feet up."

Ian lurched off the couch. "I'll get my own fucking drink, thank you!"

He staggered over toward the bar. He began rattling bottles and glasses.

"No olives," Ian protested in an eerie sort of whine. "What kind of bar is this? No olives."

"There are olives in the refrigerator," Catherine said dismissively. "Do you remember where that is? I'm going to bed."

She retrieved her book from the floor and started toward the bedroom.

"Where are you going?" Ian demanded. "Catherine, I am talking to you."

"I'm going to bed," Catherine repeated. "I'm tired and it's late."

"You can't go to bed. I'm mixing you a drink. Sit down. We'll have a drink together."

"Good night, Ian."

Once again, Catherine headed for the bedroom. In a move of sudden fury, Ian grasped her shoulder and pushed her onto the couch.

"I said sit down." His hand was hurting her shoulder. "I'm making you a nice cocktail."

"Ian, don't push me."

"Why, what are you going to do? I like pushing you. I enjoy it."

Ian was hovering over her. Catherine could
feel fright welling up in her chest.

Ian shoved his wife several times against the
back of the couch.

"For God's sake, Ian. This isn't funny. You're
hurting me. Cut it out!"

Unseen by either Ian or Catherine, the door
of Mrs. Roberts's room opened slightly. The
housekeeper's curious face popped into view.

"What you need is to relax," Ian said, suddenly jovial. "Loosen up."

"Leave me alone. I'm tired. I want to sleep."

Ian's hands went to her throat. Gripping her
by the lapels of her robe, he dragged her off
the sofa, swung her around and propelled her
toward the bar.

"I saw you the other night at the gallery," he
snarled. "You were drinking apple juice."

"Ian, please. . . ."

Ian had one hand on Catherine, the other on
a cocktail glass. "Here, have a real drink. No
apple juice in this baby."

He pushed a tumbler of gin toward her, tip-
ping it up, trying to force its contents down her
throat.

"Ian, my throat! Stop!"

Catherine tried to squirm out of his grasp.
The drink spilled onto her robe.

"Now you've made me spill it," Ian said forlornly. "I'll fix you another one."

"Don't bother."

Catherine was back on her feet. She hurried toward the bedroom.

Ian dove across the room. He tackled her and the two of them fell to the floor. Catherine tried to get up, but Ian pinned her down.

"Will you get off of me? You're being ridiculous. And stop breathing in my face. Were you drinking beer too? Goddamn you. Get off of me!"

Suddenly, Catherine slithered out of his hold. Ian looked around, puzzled. Catherine ran toward the bedroom, but Ian was too fast for her. At the entrance to the bedroom, they began to grapple.

Mrs. Roberts's face disappeared from the hall. The key turned in her bedroom lock.

Catherine was becoming furious. Ian was becoming unrecognizable.

Once Ian had pushed his wife into their bedroom, he leered at her drunkenly. "Come on, honey. I feel sexy."

Catherine drew back fearfully. "Well, I don't. I'm going to sleep in the living room."

"No, you're not. You're sleeping with me."

"What are you doing?"

"Take that robe off. Come on." Ian grinned wickedly. "I got what you want."

"How romantic," Catherine said sarcastically.

Ian pulled at her robe, tearing it open.

Underneath, Catherine was wearing only blue panties, almost boyish in style. She tried to pull away.

"You're disgusting."

Ian became enraged. He pulled off Catherine's robe. He forced her down onto the bed, pinning her under his weight. Catherine looked at him pleadingly.

"Ian, no, not like this."

"Yes, like this."

Ian commenced the procedure of sexual battery with a fury bordering on the insane.

"Ian, no, you can't," Catherine cried. She was trying to free her arms.

Ian reached down for her panties. A second later, there was the sound of fabric being torn.

Tears were streaming down Catherine's face. Her mouth was open in a quiet scream of disbelief.

"Ian, please," she finally managed to plead. "Oh, please, don't."

She struggled. Ian was too powerful for her. The more Catherine cried out and resisted, the more determined Ian became. Realizing that she could not avoid Ian's brutal form of intercourse, Catherine froze, a new fear on her face.

"Ian," she spoke through sobs. "Please listen to me. I don't have my diaphragm."

Ian was breathing heavily. "I don't care."

Catherine was completely panicked. Delirium could not be far away. "Did you hear what I said?"

Heavy breathing. The stale stink of beer and olives.

"I don't care."

Catherine continued to resist. It was no use. Ian was beyond reason.

What Ian had begun doing to Catherine might once have been characterized as intercourse. But his driving, irrational frenzy had crossed a line, making it nothing short of rape.

Frightened and repulsed, Catherine was teetering on the edge of shock. She lay on the bed woodenly, her eyes slightly glazed, her body inert, except for the movements caused by Ian's agitated thrusting.

Catherine was trying to turn off her mind like one would switch off an electric light. She struggled to reach a level at which she could remain resigned to what Ian was doing to her. How he was violating her.

Not only her body. Her mind, her soul.

Something else too.

Something that lived inside her. Beyond mind and soul.

Suddenly, Ian's movements ceased.

Catherine remained still. She tried to breathe silently. She could hear a clock ticking somewhere in the apartment. From far away, outside, a siren blared.

Ian's assault had ended. Catherine let a sigh escape from her mouth as Ian rolled off of her and collapsed onto his side of the bed.

His side of the bed.

Catherine opened her eyes. Ian was passed out on the pillow beside her, his mouth curled in a rough line, spittle dried at the corners.

Catherine felt she was looking at her husband for the very first time. His breathing was regular. His burly chest rose and fell. Catherine could not look below the waist of his body.

Incredulous at what had happened, Catherine managed to get up from the bed. A stab of pain was between her legs. Shuddering, she put her hand down there. It came away wet and bloody.

Catherine raised her hand and looked at the reddish liquid that ran along her fingers in the moonlight. Her thighs ached, her calves began to throb.

Ian's breathing sounded distressingly normal. The clock in the other room continued to tick. The ambulance siren was fading away.

Catherine picked up her robe. She put it on. She fingered the lapels, touching the fabric lovingly. She remembered the day she had bought the robe. In a store downtown that was no longer in business. It had been a bright winter day, several years earlier. Before Catherine had met the man who married her—the man who had just raped her.

Catherine closed her robe and went into the bathroom, weeping.

Chapter Nineteen

It was a dazzling day of crisp autumn colors. The sun poured its warmth over the city as if it were shielding it from harm. Or celebrating a rebirth.

The dirty, usually glum city looked remarkable, with its granite buildings gleaming, its glassworks catching the sun's rays and setting a shimmering fire to its points of color. It was as if the entire city were enchanted.

Even the seedy side of Manhattan had a bounce to its often lethargic rhythm. Prostitutes flashed their crooked smiles for a moment longer. Their pimps had a larger-than-life spring to their walk. Dope dealers, hanging out in shadowed hallways, hawked their dime bags of heroin with a bit more flash than usual. And the homeless walked with their faces turned upward to catch the momentary warmth the sun offered.

Uptown, away from all that, the mood in one apartment was decidedly different. . . .

"Don't ever do that again. If you do, I'll kill you."

It was the morning after the rape, at about ten o'clock. The sun streamed into the Bishop master bedroom. Ian had just stirred and opened his eyes.

Catherine stood at the foot of the bed. She was fully dressed. Her hair looked radiant in the creeping sunlight.

Catherine looked down at the groggy Ian with an air of clinical detachment. Once again, when she spoke, her voice was cold and clipped.

"Did you hear me, Ian? If you ever do that again, you're dead."

"I don't know how I had the courage to say that. I mean I threatened to kill him. I've never stood up to Ian that way before."

The late afternoon sun glowed on the rug of Janet Parker's office. The doctor sat across from Catherine, a memo pad open on her lap. Occasionally, she made some notes on its lined pages. Catherine looked distraught.

"How do you feel about that?" Janet asked her.

"Well, after he attacked me, all I could feel

was a kind of rage. I felt used. Ian raped me. I stayed up all night thinking about that."

"But you knew he was drunk."

"Yes."

Janet Parker engaged her client's eyes. "Do you think you can excuse Ian because he was drunk?"

Catherine looked away. "No." She paused. "I'm not sure. I know this much. I'll never allow myself to be used like that again."

Janet wrote some words on her lined notepad. "Do you think what Ian did to you was a criminal offense?"

"Do you mean am I going to press charges? No, of course not." Catherine sounded almost indignant.

"Well, what happens now? Do you think you can go on living with Ian?"

Catherine sighed. "He's my husband."

"What about your sex life? Is this going to change things?"

"It has to, don't you think?"

"That's up to you and Ian. Maybe in time things will get back to the way they were. You don't look convinced."

"I'm not," Catherine admitted. There was regret and defiance in her tone.

Catherine closed her eyes for a moment. She leaned her head back in the chair. Janet studied her.

"What about Bobo?" the psychologist asked gently. "What does he think?"

Catherine's eyes opened suddenly. When she spoke, she sounded forced and rehearsed.

"Bobo?" A faint laugh escaped Catherine's lips. "Dr. Parker, I know Bobo is imaginary. He isn't real. Bobo's in my head. I made him up. How can Bobo think anything?"

Catherine was still. Janet looked at her client skeptically. A gulf was opening between them.

In the elevator, on the way down from her session, Catherine was alone.

She stood in a corner, her arms folded protectively in front of her. Her voice was hoarse, urgent, an eerie whisper that sounded at once like a girlish confession and the dry crackle of dead leaves rustling.

"I told her you weren't real. I had to lie to her. I think she believed me. You're safe now, Bobo. No one else is going to interfere. It's just you and me."

Catherine giggled. The floors sped by through the small window in the elevator door. Catherine was going down quickly.

Weeks later, a doctor confirmed what Catherine had suspected since the rape.

Catherine was pregnant.

Part II

BOBO

Chapter Twenty

The Evil had waited far too long. At last, its time to infiltrate man had come. It teased, cajoled and, in some cases, forced its way into the very souls of men. Somewhere, the scales were tipped in its favor. The Evil began to outweigh good. It could be heard laughing in the rustling of a hot desert wind, the sudden clap of thunder on a cloudless night, the maniacal chuckling of a madman. And the population grew.

The weather was going to change. There was an approaching storm creeping in from the north. You could see nature's way of preparing for the onslaught. You could see these hints if you looked very closely.

The insect world knew of the storm. The

diminutive creatures scrambled about in a frenzy, buzzing and humming in their language. The dry grass seemed to stand up stiffly as though waiting for the first drops of moisture to relieve its thirst.

The first splatter of rain was preceded by a cold north wind, pushing large swollen clouds into a mass that turned the daytime sky slate gray. The downpour drove most people indoors. The ones taken by surprise quickly found shelter. There was an unmistakable wrongness about the storm.

Perhaps it was the unexpected lightning slicing the dark December sky with strips of brilliant color. Or perhaps it was the dusky warmth—unnatural for that time of the year. Perhaps it was the way the storm ended. Suddenly.

The sun shoved its way through the dense cloud covering as if to show it was the winner of some macabre contest of nature. One minute after the storm ceased, the moisture on the ground was almost completely dried. Only the trees, still heavy with raindrops, drooped toward the earth.

Still, there was something in the air.

In a room in a swollen apartment project in the desolate section of the South Bronx, an old East African man who practiced voodoo shivered in his threadbare clothes at what might be coming. In a deserted subway tunnel near Grand Central Station, a crippled derelict who heard voices in his head murmured unnamed fears into a rusty metal grating. Down on a quiet street in Greenwich Village, an eccentric seer who had emigrated to this country from her native Russia might have foretold something dreadful that was coming in on wings of evil, if only she had still been alive.

On Fifth Avenue, along the edge of Central Park, two figures walked, oblivious to the storm that had come and gone, leaving them still entangled in their halting conversation. The taller figure had his arm around his companion. She looked small and vulnerable in the flickering sunlight, which played like splashing diamonds on the passing windshields.

The couple approached the fountain in front of the Plaza Hotel, but the happy clamor of Christmas shoppers drove them westward along the park's southern rim.

Catherine leaned closer to her husband. "Ian, I'm scared. My mother died having a baby."

"That was a long time ago," Ian said, his gruff voice strangely muted in the busy roar of crosstown traffic.

"I don't care. I'm frightened."

"People don't die in childbirth anymore. You're going to have the best care that money can buy. The best doctors. The best hospital. I'll see to all of that."

"I know. I can't help it. I just have this feeling something is going to go wrong."

"Nothing will go wrong. You're healthy. You're twenty-five years old. It'll be fine. I promise."

Catherine glanced sideways wistfully. "I read every day about women having abortions."

Ian looked away. "I don't want to hear about abortion."

"I know. I could never do that. But when I got that paper from the lab telling me I was pregnant, the thought did cross my mind."

"There's something else, isn't there?"

Catherine hesitated. "I can't help thinking about that night. I warned you that it wasn't safe. I know that's the night I got pregnant."

"You don't know that," Ian replied, trimming the edge from his voice with a conscious effort. "Since when is the diaphragm one hundred percent effective?"

"It always was before."

"Look, I'm sorry about that night. I've apologized a thousand times."

Catherine didn't answer. A bit uneasy, Ian stopped. From off in the distance, an ambulance siren sent up its loud insistent cry.

"I've got an idea," Ian said. "How would you like to spend some time on Nantucket?"

Catherine looked at her husband. There was a wariness in her eyes. "Nantucket?"

"I hear it's beautiful in the winter," Ian rushed on, his words clinging to one another. "You've got the house now. I could fly up on weekends. You can take Mrs. Roberts with you. There's a medical center right on the island. You can have regular checkups. The clean air will be good for you. Maybe Laura can come up for a visit. Didn't you tell me there were some shops on Nantucket where you can sell your dolls?"

Head down, Catherine pawed the toe of her boot in a clump of grass that was struggling to survive in the sidewalk. "It is nice there in the winter. Like a picture postcard."

"It's a great idea!" Ian said enthusiastically. "It'll be the perfect place for you. You'll be able to paint, take walks, whatever you want to do. You're always saying you never have enough time by yourself, right?"

"It would be nice," Catherine admitted softly. "Yeah, I think I'd like that."

"It'll be an adventure. You'll be mistress of the island."

"Just like when I was a kid," Catherine replied, her voice barely audible in the suddenly still air. An odd smile played at the corners of her mouth.

"Exactly!"

Catherine's reply was a whisper that never reached her husband's ears.

"With Bobo."

Chapter Twenty-One

"So what are we going to do on New Year's Eve? We can't have a party without you."

"Oh, that's sweet, Laura."

It was two days before Christmas. Catherine was on the floor of her living room in front of a small decorated tree. She was packing art supplies, blank doll heads and other items of her profession into a large cardboard crate. Seated on the nearby sofa, Laura Spinoza was having a mug of holiday eggnog.

"I'm lucky Ian's letting me stay for Christmas," Catherine said. "He wanted to leave immediately. He's got Nantucket fever."

"He'd better have Nantucket fever. You two are going to freeze your butts off up there."

"Hand me those books, will you?"

Laura passed her friend a small stack of art books. Catherine began packing them into the crate.

"What about you?"

Catherine looked up. "What do you mean?"

"Do you have Nantucket fever?"

"I've always had Nantucket fever. Now I'm going to have Nantucket fever and morning sickness all at once. That should be fun."

"Not everyone gets morning sickness. You might be one of the lucky ones."

Catherine raised folded hands to the heavens in mock seriousness. "Oh, God, let me be one of the lucky ones!"

"My, aren't we coping?"

"Am I coping?" Catherine asked in an almost puzzled tone. "Oh, good."

Laura studied her friend for a moment before speaking. "You're not frightened?"

"I am frightened. I've never been so scared in my life."

"You want this baby."

"Yes," Catherine agreed softly. "I've always wanted a baby. It's *having* a baby that terrifies me."

"You'll be just fine," Laura said reassuringly.

Catherine reached for a box. From it she took the malevolent child doll. Laura's necklace still hung from its neck. Lovingly, Catherine began to wrap the doll, giving it a place of honor in her suitcase.

Laura looked wary. "You're not taking him to Nantucket, are you?"

"I know. He gives you the creeps. But I painted him and I think he's beautiful."

"I think he's spooky."

Catherine looked at her strangely. "I wouldn't dream of going away without him. He's my friend."

Late afternoon of Christmas Eve, Janet Parker was working in her office when Ian phoned.

"I'm calling about Catherine," he said brusquely.

"Merry Christmas, Mr. Bishop."

"Yes, well, I won't keep you. I just wanted to tell you Catherine won't be coming for any more of your sessions. My wife is pregnant and I'm taking her out of the city for a few months."

Janet was momentarily taken aback. "Do you think that's a good idea? Catherine and I have been making very good progress, Mr. Bishop."

"I've heard about your progress. Listen, I told my wife to see you because she was having nightmares. Well, the nightmares have stopped."

"Yes," Janet began, "but there's more to it than that. We've gotten into other areas."

"Like imaginary playmates. I know all about it. That's stopped as well."

"I'm not so sure about that. Catherine says it has stopped."

151

"*I* say it has stopped." Ian was annoyed. "Catherine's all right now. She's going to be a mother. I'm taking her away to Nantucket. She loves it there."

"Mr. Bishop," Janet said in alarm, "that's the last place in the world you should take her."

"What are you talking about?"

"You're taking her to the very house that she had nightmares about. Her childhood was upsetting. You shouldn't put her back there."

"Is that so?"

"It's unhealthy."

"Are you telling me what to do?"

"It could trigger something off."

"That's ridiculous."

"It's not ridiculous. I know more about this than you do. Your wife isn't well. She may be more deeply disturbed than you realize."

"Dr. Parker, I appreciate your concern. You see my wife for two hours a week. I spend a great deal more time with her. I think I know Catherine pretty well. You say she's disturbed. I'll be the judge of that."

"Could I speak with her?"

"That's not necessary. I'm speaking for her. Merry Christmas, Dr. Parker."

"Just let me. . . ."

Ian hung up. With a worried look, Janet replaced the receiver. A cold wind seemed to rustle the room. Janet shivered with a newfound dread.

Chapter Twenty-Two

Even for the end of December, it was unseasonably cold on the stretch of water that separated Nantucket from the mainland of Massachusetts. The sun looked pale, as if it were giving out only half of its available rays. The sky was cloudless, reflecting on the ocean, which appeared a cold and hostile blue.

The ferry from Woods Hole was nearing the completion of its run. More than an hour earlier, it had docked to let off passengers at Martha's Vineyard and now what Catherine always thought of as the "sturdier travelers"—those bound for Nantucket, another 20 miles out to sea—were approaching their destination.

Wrapped up against the cold, Catherine stood alone at the bow of the ship. Behind her, in the enclosed portion of the ferry, Ian sat with Mrs. Roberts, each of them taking turns at glancing toward the deck to . . . to what? Catherine wondered. To see if she would fall overboard? She could feel their looks bore into her from time to time like the revolving beam of a prison beacon.

Catherine felt exhilarated. She had been on the deck for nearly an hour, her eyes searching the horizon restlessly for her childhood home. Looking to the land, Catherine could see activity on the beach and along the low rocky promontories that ringed the island. Seagulls stood in bunches, quiet, waiting. The sound of the waves crashing against the rocks struggled to overcome the roar of the wind as the ship cruised toward the island, like a smooth car on a highway.

From time to time, a bird would take flight from the shore as though, Catherine imagined, suddenly frightened by something. There was a pungent aroma riding on the frigid wind. A stench of decay and something more distasteful—something old and unnameable.

Once the ferry had docked at the weathered end of Nantucket's main street, Catherine wasted no time in going ashore. As Ian and Mrs. Roberts struggled down the gangplank carrying suitcases, Catherine walked briskly ahead of them. She hugged herself excitedly. She threw back her head in delight. The wind rushed through her hair. Cold. Invigorating. Familiar.

She was home.

*   *   *

"It's coming up soon, just around this turn."

Catherine leaned forward in the passenger seat of the rented car. Beside her, Ian was peering through the windshield, carefully negotiating the wooded curves that lead to the Bellamy house of Catherine's childhood.

Behind them, low in the back seat, Mrs. Roberts sat, her face a resolute mask.

"Now, Ian, right after those trees. . . ."

Catherine let out a cry of excitement. The Bellamy house rose up before them, looking unchanged from years earlier, still majestic against the flinty winter sky and the out-thrust branches of the nearby woods.

The house was white, two-storied, distinguished in front by four Doric columns of majestic stature. The two interior pillars framed a double door of chestnut wood adorned with knobs of brilliant silver.

Each of the high casement windows, on both the first and second floor, was set off by handsome shutters of a rich midnight blue. Towering over all were the house's eaves, each with a small dormer window. Surrounded by the eaves was the building's railed observation platform, the rectangular widow's walk, named for the wives of whalers who, according to tradition, paced there while their husbands were at sea.

*   *   *

The elegant bedroom once occupied by Catherine's father was as impressive as she remembered. It retained its antique charm and sense of masculine mystery.

Ian and Catherine stood in the doorway. Ian put his arm protectively around his wife.

Catherine's mind was beginning to drift. After a moment, she disengaged herself from Ian. She crossed the room and stared at the bed, which was covered by a thick, blue quilt.

Catherine walked quietly to the adjacent bathroom. Ian's eyes followed her. Ian held his breath.

Tentatively, like a little child, Catherine entered the bathroom. It looked essentially the same as when her father had slashed himself there.

Catherine approached the mirror. She looked intently at the glass, almost as though expecting to see the reflection of a frightened girl.

Quietly, Ian came up behind her.

Catherine turned. Ian was staring into the mirror. Catherine touched his arm. She tried to smile.

"I'm okay, Ian."

Chapter Twenty-Three

Time passed on the island. Once again, Catherine found herself settling into Nantucket's remote, natural rhythm.

The winds. The way sounds traveled at night. The waves. Faraway lights on the horizon. New boats at the wharf in the morning. Old boats gone without warning.

The cold. More biting every day. Yet more familiar.

Catherine worked every day. What had once been her bedroom was gradually converted into her studio. Once she was comfortable, she spent time alone, painting her doll faces. She seemed relaxed and healthy.

In the corner of the room, watching her every movement, the malevolent child doll waited. . . .

*   *   *

Catherine went regularly to a nearby clinic, where she was examined by a Dr. Bernard. He was a young obstetrician, still single, who wondered why this attractive young woman never was accompanied to checkups by a male companion.

Catherine scarcely noticed Dr. Bernard's kindly, even solicitous concern. She was growing comfortable with her role as a mother-to-be.

One morning at the clinic, after Catherine had gotten dressed, she mentioned Ian in passing. Later, she left the one-story building and walked gingerly down the snow-covered steps to her car. When she drove off, Dr. Bernard watched until her car disappeared, then smoked a cigarette in dull silence.

Catherine found a store in town that would stock her dolls. It was called Trudy's Trifles and was run by a woman called Mary Belinda, who couldn't tell her who Trudy was or even if there was a Trudy. Catherine didn't really care if such a woman existed. The shop, which was cluttered with a variety of handmade items, figurines, sachets, silk flowers, and greeting cards, would be featuring Catherine's creations. Mary Belinda gave her a check for a modest amount in exchange for five dolls and Catherine smiled graciously. Nantucket could be lovely. People had always told her that.

Animus

*   *   *

Catherine bought maternity outfits and tried them on, admiring herself in a full-length mirror.

Time hurried by.

Months had passed since she had been in New York. It seemed like some distant town from an old movie.

When Ian called, Catherine, dressed in an ample robe now, sounded almost carefree.

"Ian, I'm fine. You don't have to come up every weekend. Why don't you come for Easter?"

A week later, Catherine lay on her bed, on top of the blankets, staring at the ceiling. Suddenly, she gave a start. She grinned.

"It moved," she said excitedly. "The baby's kicking."

She felt her stomach.

"Put your hand here, Bobo. You can feel it!"

Ian couldn't make it on Easter weekend. Catherine scarcely noticed. Ian turned up a week later and the two of them walked along the beach.

Catherine was quite heavy, but she walked briskly enough. She wanted to keep up with her husband and she did.

Ian had an arm around her waist, but Catherine kept breaking loose to pick up seashells, collecting the pretty ones in a shoulder bag.

Bobo will like these.

"You're not upset?"

Ian looked earnestly into his wife's eyes. The two of them were seated at a corner table in Elia's, a candle-lit Nantucket restaurant.

"Upset?" Catherine asked, staring into her after-dinner coffee. "Do I look upset?"

"No," Ian admitted. "It's just that I said I'd be up here on weekends and, well, you know, with the new gallery. . . . Andrew Garron's turning into a superstar."

"As you predicted he would," Catherine noted.

"Yes, but. . . ."

Catherine smiled. She waved her hand dismissively.

"Ian, I'm perfectly fine. I like being alone. I know you're busy. If I need anything, Mrs. Roberts is always there. She's really always there. She's practically underfoot."

"I could have a word with her," Ian said, looking contrite. "If she's bothersome. . . ."

"No," Catherine laughed. "It's just her nature. She's been around too long to change."

Ian gazed across the candle-lit table, admiring his wife. "You look wonderful."

"I feel good. I keep waiting for something to happen."

Catherine paused.

"Maybe your guardian angel is looking after you," Ian suggested.

Catherine's eyes twinkled. She smiled enigmatically.

"Maybe he is."

Chapter Twenty-Four

The Evil devised ways of killing in numbers. It was delighted when man conceived the notion of holy wars. So many thousands died then. It was particularly pleased to see the one who called Himself the Son of God meet His end in such a barbaric way. The Evil had thought Jesus would make a good assistant. It had tried to convert Him. But Jesus fought the Evil and died suffering for the people's sins. It wasn't long before armies grew and bloodthirsty generals led their troops in fighting senseless wars. Wars served the needs of the Evil. Especially as weapons grew more sophisticated. Thousands could die in just minutes.

Timewise, Nantucket continued to work its

charm. Days seemed endless, wrapped in cold spring breezes and the remnants of snow. Nights were for the fireside, clothed in warm robes and blankets, with hot tea always at one's fingertips. Yet, for all the tranquillity and even lethargy, the weeks flowed into one another. Spring stood guard against summer, but it was a foolish watch. It was nearly June.

Outside the window of the Bellamy kitchen, robins and bluebirds chirped. The lilacs were already budding. Inside, Catherine and Mrs. Roberts were busy baking bread in the kitchen's austere, old-fashioned oven.

The kitchen was newly painted. Catherine had discovered a delicate yellow to her liking and had done the job herself. Coupled with the south wall, which was of exposed brick, the effect was cheerful, even optimistic.

Mrs. Roberts was basting a roast that Tuesday morning. An elaborate salad was being prepared by Catherine, who hummed softly as she chopped peppers.

The housekeeper eyed her sideways. She'd like me to think she's normal, Mrs. Roberts decided, but I must watch her.

Later that afternoon, Catherine, wearing a summery maternity dress, came along the cliff walk. The sun was blindingly bright. The wind was brisk.

Catherine halted. She looked down at the water that crashed inexorably on the beach.

The waves crested to impossible heights, then caved in on themselves. They rushed toward the shore, brushing the sand, quickly changing direction, then washing back out to sea. Birds flew in sweeping circles, diving toward the ocean, skimming the surface, then taking flight seconds before they would have collided with the waves.

Catherine smiled, seeing the rows of small boats that bobbed like corks in the harbor. Her hair was ruffled. Her expression was almost manic. She spoke in a girlish, singsong cadence.

"Bobo? It's almost time. The doctor says any day now. What am I going to do?" She paused. "How? How are you going to be here? Ian is going to be here. I told Ian you don't exist. What happens when I'm having the baby? You have to be there. Don't let anything happen to me, Bobo, please. . . ."

Catherine paused again. A reply to her plea was echoing inside her mind.

She smiled, looking reassured, as though a great weight had been lifted from her.

The Fleet taxi, driven by 75-year-old Roy West, a lifelong resident of the island, sped along the two-lane blacktop past a cemetery whose ancient headstones practically leaned against one another.

"Look at that old graveyard!" Laura Spinoza cried from the back seat of the cab.

"Seen it," Roy answered brusquely, puffing on a Lucky Strike. It was his first comment since picking Laura up at the ferry.

"Yes, of course you have. It looks like one of those graveyards from a horror movie. Like it might be haunted."

"Wouldn't surprise me."

"I'm not from around here," Laura offered.

Roy squinted at the rearview mirror. "Didn't think so."

"But you'd never catch me in that graveyard. Not after dark, anyway."

"Fraidy cat, huh?" Roy took a corner with his eyes closed.

"I suppose so."

"You come to the wrong place then. Nantucket's not for fraidy cats."

"No?"

"Too much history. Too many shipwrecks. Too many widows left alone. Too many kids with dead pappies. Too many sounds in the night. See those gravestones? How they can't stand up straight? Like the corpses are trying to come up from six feet under."

Laura shuddered. "You're scaring me."

Roy shook his head sadly. "No place for fraidy cats."

Soon, the Bellamy house appeared in the cab's front window. Laura let out a tiny sigh of relief.

The taxi pulled up into the front drive. Laura got out and was immediately greeted by Mrs.

Roberts, who had spotted her from the side garden.

Roy West got Laura's two suitcases out of the trunk. As Laura was paying him, she glanced up toward the nearby cliff. Catherine was waving to her.

As large cumulus clouds rolled across the sky, Catherine made her way down toward the house, walking in their shadow.

Roy got back into his taxi. He smiled at the cute young New York woman and drove off.

The Bellamy living room was large, beam-ceilinged and very comfortable, with a wood-burning fireplace. Catherine had decorated it with numerous quilts and throw rugs, giving it a lively, informal air.

After telling her friend about her peculiar cab ride, Laura was beginning to feel refreshed from her journey. Catherine had shown no reaction to Laura's taxi anecdote. Indeed, she seemed a little detached.

"Ian was over for dinner the other night," Laura said, sipping her vodka gimlet.

"Oh?" Catherine sounded far away.

"He and Michael were going to the Yankee game." Laura studied her friend. "He misses you."

"Ian will be here soon enough," Catherine said in a clipped tone. "Not that he has to hurry. The doctor says I've got at least another ten days."

"Have you decided on a name?"

"If it's a girl, I'd like to name her Julia—after my mother."

"And if it's a boy?"

"Julian."

"I'm surprised that Ian doesn't want to name it after some post-modern painter."

"It's my baby," Catherine said coldly. "I'll name it anything I want."

Mrs. Roberts came softly into the room. "Dinner's ready."

Catherine spoke almost as if the other women were not there.

"I was out on the cliff today, looking down at the waves. I felt reassured. I don't think I'm going to be afraid. An old friend of mine is going to see me through."

Puzzled, Laura looked across at Mrs. Roberts. The old housekeeper turned away.

That night, clouds obscured the moon. Laura was on the porch swing reading a paperback by the light of a small table lamp. She'd been lost in the book since finishing dinner. It was almost eleven o'clock.

A breeze stirred the porch screen, rattling it slightly in its moorings. Something flickered just outside Laura's line of sight. She put down her book and blinked her eyes back to reality.

Off to the side of the porch, the light had gone out in Catherine's studio. Seconds later, a flickering was seen from the same window.

Curious, Laura put down her book. She went out on the porch steps and listened. Then she walked toward the window of Catherine's studio.

Drawing closer, she could see into the room. She hesitated, then peered through the glass.

Catherine was lying on the studio couch, her eyes staring vacantly at the ceiling. The flickering candle she had just lit sent her shadow dancing on the nearby wall and ceiling.

Catherine was speaking. Laura frowned, trying to decipher what her friend was saying.

Through the window, she could see Catherine turn to the malevolent boy doll that was perched impishly on the shelf near her head.

A little bit closer and Laura might be able to hear what she was saying.

Laura leaned toward the window. The moonlight, streaming down from above, seemed to illuminate her as though she were caught in a floodlight. Then Laura could hear her friend's words, uttered in a rhythmic, chantlike way.

"They don't know who you are. They don't see you like I do. They can't feel you like I can. You're just for me. Ian thinks he's just for me. But Ian doesn't know."

Laura listened, but there was no more. Suddenly, her concern for Catherine gave way to something else. A deathly fear like nothing she had ever known.

Chapter Twenty-Five

"You sold all nine? That's terrific."

It was the next morning. Across the breakfast table from Laura, Catherine was talking on the phone to the proprietor of the doll shop.

"Oh, my goodness," Catherine went on. "Yes, I can let you have five more."

Catherine paused as the other party spoke. At the stove, Mrs. Roberts looked up from scrambling some eggs.

"What does being pregnant have to do with it?" Catherine wanted to know. "I can still paint. I'll tell you what. I'll bring down three of them this afternoon. You can have the others next week."

Catherine hung up the phone. She took a sip of coffee and smiled at Laura.

"Congratulations," Laura said.

"Nine dolls sold in the last two weeks. I never sold them that fast in New York. Who's buying them?"

"Probably New Yorkers," Laura said.

Catherine's grin widened. "You're probably right. They come up here, they buy them!"

"I saw your light on last night," Laura said matter-of-factly. "Were you working?"

Mrs. Roberts served the scrambled eggs from the frying pan. She was listening to the conversation.

"For a while, yes, I was working. Why?"

"I was sitting on the porch, reading. I thought I heard you talking to somebody."

Catherine said nothing.

"Were you on the phone?"

"No," Catherine replied.

"I thought maybe Ian called."

Catherine nibbled on her toast. "I wasn't talking to anyone. You must have imagined it."

"She talks to herself. She's been doing it for at least a year now."

Mrs. Roberts and Laura were walking along the beach. It was midafternoon of the same day.

"I didn't mean to eavesdrop," Laura explained. "It's just that it was . . . scary."

"I shouldn't really say she talks to herself," the housekeeper went on, seemingly oblivious to Laura's last remark. "She talks to somebody named Bobo."

"Bobo? That's the name she mentioned at the gallery the night she touched the painting."

Mrs. Roberts looked far out to sea. "At first, I thought it was one of her dolls. But I've heard her do it when there weren't any dolls around. I heard her talking to Bobo late, alone in her bedroom. There aren't any dolls in there."

"Exactly what are you saying?"

"I'm not saying anything." Mrs. Roberts sounded defensive. "What people do in their bedrooms is their business. But when Mr. Bishop isn't around, I hear her talk to this Bobo. That's not all I hear."

Laura stopped walking.

"Go on, Mrs. Roberts."

"It's unnatural."

"Have you spoken to Mr. Bishop?"

"Would you? The first time I heard her talking to this Bobo, it was all quite innocent. Still, I mentioned it to Mr. Bishop. He didn't want to hear about it."

"My God. She's been doing this for a year?"

Mrs. Roberts nodded. "Actually, it's gotten a lot worse since she's been on the island."

"I think Ian ought to know about this."

Mrs. Roberts gave Laura a wise smile. "Then you ought to tell him."

Chapter Twenty-Six

The sun, hunkered down on the horizon, blazed with a fiery anger. On the verge of setting, it seemed to roll for a moment, like a feverish eye about to be extinguished.

Laura stood at the gate, watching as the two-engine plane approached the airport runway. She felt anxious as the 12-seater aircraft touched down, and almost frightened as the small door at the airplane's side opened and Ian's husky bulk appeared.

Ian walked purposefully toward her. He gave her a perfunctory kiss on the cheek and waved toward a Nantucket cab driver who was reading a racing form nearby.

Five minutes later, as the taxi approached the Bellamy house, Laura still had misgivings.

"I feel funny about this," she finally admitted to Ian.

"You did the right thing," Ian countered with a grim smile. "I'm glad you called me. I've got nothing better to do than fly up here on a moment's notice to look at Catherine's latest routine. God, what some women won't do for attention!"

"I'm not sure she's doing it for attention. I mean, I heard her. She really believes that something is there."

Ian sighed. "Something called Bobo. I know all about it. I've warned Catherine. This time she's gone too far."

Ian glared out the car window. Laura was suddenly very scared for her friend.

The cab stopped in front of the Bellamy house. Ian jumped out of the back seat and ran up the front steps, leaving Laura to fumble in her purse for money to pay the driver.

Ian opened the front door and went into the house. Once inside the living room, he looked around impatiently.

"Catherine?" he called out.

Hearing no reply, Ian strode down the corridor toward his wife's studio. He pushed open the door angrily.

The force of the door opening dislodged a shelf from the wall of Catherine's room. The shelf crashed to the floor, sending doll parts rolling across the carpet.

Ian jumped back, startled.

"Catherine?" His voice was angry now.

Ian ventured farther into the room. He looked around quickly. No sign of Catherine.

Ian emerged from the studio. He hurried down the hallway toward the master bedroom. Halfway there, he began to hear Catherine's voice. It was private, little more than a murmur. It came in a singsong rhythm. Ian could not make out the words.

The door to the Bellamy master bedroom was open. Ian went into the room, moving slowly. His eyes took in the bedroom, darting about furiously.

The room was neat. A comforter covered the large double bed. Next to the bed, on a night table, was a framed wedding photo of Ian and Catherine.

Ian came to a halt. His eyes bore holes into the picture in its silver frame.

The photo had been dramatically altered. Someone, using red crayon, had drawn a comical beard and mustache on Ian's face. Ian thought he knew who that someone was.

Ian's anger was mounting. He struggled to blend it with an intuitive caution as he moved through the bedroom toward a bright shaft of light.

Ian approached the source of light, the bathroom, the door of which was slightly ajar. Catherine's voice was heard once again. Louder, this time. Still in a singsong, but Ian could make out the words:

Animus

"I am my dolly.
My dolly is me.
Bobo loves dolly.
And Bobo loves me."

Gently, Ian pushed the bathroom door open. He looked inside. He could see Catherine standing in front of the bathroom mirror, but he could not see her face. Propped up on the sink was the malevolent boy doll, dressed in a black tuxedo.

Ian moved closer. Catherine was unaware of Ian's presence. Catherine herself wore an oversize tuxedo jacket. Ian recognized it as one of his own coats. Catherine was applying makeup to her face. Ian drew nearer, but Catherine's hand obscured her face from him.

Catherine's voice continued its singsong chant, barely above a whisper.

"I love my dolly.
My dolly is me.
I love Bobo.
And Bobo loves me."

Ian was stunned. For several seconds, he found himself unable to move. Then he hurled himself into the bathroom and swung Catherine roughly around. Ian stared at her face. "Oh, Jesus Christ," he moaned.

Catherine's face was made up exactly like that of the malevolent boy doll.

The eyebrows—arched and tapered nearly down to the cheekbones.

The eyes—long-lashed, caked in grotesque purple and black.

The nose—lined in red, with paintlike blood seeming to drip from each nostril.

The cheeks—rouged in mocking stars and half-moons.

The mouth—distended, maroon, like a bruised gash.

The teeth—blackened in taunting evil like a devil child's jack-o'-lantern.

Seeing Ian, she smiled maniacally.

"Are you crazy?" Ian hollered. "Do you know what you look like?"

Catherine's eyes were lit by a glossy madness. Her voice recited in childlike fashion:

"I am my dolly.
My dolly is me."

Catherine tilted her head back. She laughed giddily. Her eyes danced crazily. "Hi, Ian."

Ian ripped the tuxedo jacket from her chest. He bunched up the sleeve of the ripped garment and started vigorously rubbing at her face. Catherine struggled to pull herself away, but Ian persisted.

"I never should have left you alone up here," Ian said, as though talking to himself.

Catherine spun away from his grasp. "I hav-

176

en't been alone." Hands on hips, she grinned slyly. "You-know-who is here."

"Take off that makeup. You're going back to New York."

Catherine giggled. "I don't wanna go nowhere. I'm staying right here."

Catherine picked up the child doll and tucked it protectively under her arm. She started out of the bathroom.

Ian, enraged, tore the doll from Catherine's grasp. He hurled it against the bathroom wall. The doll bounced and landed in the bathtub. Catherine burst into tears of hysteria.

"No!" she screamed, tearing at Ian's shirt. She tried to dive toward the bathtub, but Ian tightened his grip on her. He dragged her from the bathroom.

Back in the bedroom, Ian maneuvered her over toward the bed. Catherine continued to struggle as Ian deposited her on the bed. She tried to get up, but he pushed her back down.

Mrs. Roberts and Laura were standing in the bedroom doorway. Ian, on his way to the bathroom for a washcloth, spied them. He turned around and glared.

"Stay out of this, both of you."

Ian bounded across the room. He pushed the bedroom door shut in their astonished faces.

Retrieving a washcloth from the sink, Ian began to rub the paint from Catherine's face. She tried to resist. Her tears only caused the makeup to run more. Her face looked like a rain-splattered canvas.

"We're getting the next flight back to New York," Ian muttered as he rubbed away at the paint. "I don't care if I have to drag you out of here. Hold still."

Ian had gotten most of the paint off. He yanked Catherine to her feet and shoved her toward the bathroom.

"Wash your face," he ordered. "We're getting out of here. Move!"

Catherine remained where she was. Slowly, she sat back down on the bed. Her body went limp. Once again, she spoke in a childish whimper.

"You hurt dolly. Bobo's mad."

"Don't start with that shit, Catherine."

Ian pulled her to a standing position. Catherine slipped from his grasp, lost her balance and started to fall.

Ian tried to catch her, but it was too late. The pregnant woman fell heavily to the floor, landing on her stomach.

Catherine's face was suddenly contorted with pain.

"Oh, God, Ian. The baby!"

Catherine let out an unearthly scream. The door burst open. Laura and Mrs. Roberts rushed in.

Ian stood there in shock, staring down at his wife. Catherine squirmed in agony on the floor.

"She's gone into labor!" Laura shrieked in alarm.

Minutes later, the Bishop family car was careening down a two-lane blacktop road, headed for the hospital. Behind the wheel, Ian was driving with a recklessness that had him taking curves almost on two wheels, cutting off other vehicles and narrowly missing a fence post at the side of the road.

Sweat matted on his forehead, Ian stared fixedly through the windshield at the road. Beside him on the front seat was a shrieking Catherine. Next to her, trying to comfort her friend was Laura, looking scared to death.

"It'll be okay," Laura said soothingly. "We're almost there."

She leaned over to mop sweat from Catherine's brow. With smeared paint on her face, Catherine had a tragic look. She continued screaming. She was beyond even hearing Laura.

Laura glanced over at Ian. Her look was almost one of accusation.

When the Bishop car screeched to a stop at the front door of the hospital, attendants were already racing down the steps. Catherine was helped from the car onto a stretcher. The attendants carried her into the hospital. Laura ran up the steps after them. A dazed Ian followed.

A half hour later, Ian and Laura were alone

in the waiting room. Ian paced nervously.

"What happened?" Laura finally asked. "What did you do to her?"

Ian looked away. "She fell. I swear to God. She fell. I didn't touch her. She fell. . . ."

His voice trailed off hopelessly.

Chapter Twenty-Seven

The Evil inhabited the one called Hitler and millions died. That was one of the rare times it felt happiness. The Evil was most content when the chaos and destruction it caused was done as a human being. But what the Evil longed for was to manifest into a human—not to simply go inside one and use the body like a puppet. The Evil wanted to be born. It wanted to be what it was and walk as a man. And, even with all its power, that could not be. Not for millions of years. Not until the end of the Twentieth century. Then it was time. . . .

In the operating wing of the hospital, behind doors marked *Authorized Personnel Only,* Catherine lay on a table, her legs in stirrups, surrounded by her young obstetrician, several nurses and two interns who had come over from Hyannis Port just that morning.

Catherine was awake, but just barely. Her eyes were glazed from tranquilizers. Dr. Bernard leaned over. He spoke quietly into her ear.

"Catherine, we've administered a local anesthetic. That should cut down on the pain. Now we need your help. You have to push. Do you hear what I'm saying?"

Catherine nodded. Dr. Bernard turned to his aides.

"I think we're ready."

Given the nature of what was inside Catherine, the birth began smoothly enough.

After 66 minutes, and half a dozen seconds, the baby's head began to emerge.

"That's fine, Catherine," Dr. Bernard said enthusiastically. "Here it comes."

Catherine's body arched. Her eyes rolled crazily in her head. Sweat poured down her face.

"Now push!" Dr. Bernard shouted.

The baby came out still farther. Catherine's body jerked in a spasm. A gusher of blood shot out of her, followed by another, twice as powerful.

Dr. Bernard turned anxiously to one of the nurses.

"She's hemorrhaging. We'll have to put her out."

"No!" Catherine screamed.

All eyes were on the emerging baby. Its head. The nurses frowned. The interns from the mainland stepped back in astonishment, their faces drained of blood.

Push. Push. Out came the baby's head. The umbilical cord was wrapped in a stranglehold around the baby's throat. Blood gushed out as though from a faucet.

Catherine was twisting and throbbing on the table. She screamed horribly. A nurse was trying to put the anesthetic mask over her face.

Dr. Bernard pulled the blood-drenched baby out of Catherine. He cut the cord from its neck, freeing it from its unholy garrote.

He handed the baby to a nurse. She tried to detect a heartbeat.

"I can't get a beat," the nurse cried. She shook her head and looked at the doctor helplessly.

The other nurse had succeeded in fitting the anesthetic over Catherine's mouth.

Catherine wriggled free of it. Blood came out of her mouth, where she had bitten her tongue, her lips.

An eerie whisper came from Catherine.

"Bobo, you promised."

A pause. Catherine shrieked in desperation. "Bobo!"

Catherine's head jerked back onto the pillow. The mask came over her face and was clasped into place.

Dr. Bernard and the others were working frantically to stop the hemorrhaging that was flooding the operating table with Catherine's blood.

"She's going into cardiac arrest!" one of the nurses screamed.

At the side of the table, the machine that recorded the patient's pulse rate showed Catherine's heartbeat starting to falter.

Dr. Bernard was looking in astonishment—at something else. Something entirely unexpected.

From between Catherine Bishop's legs, another baby's head was beginning to emerge.

"My God, it's twins!"

It was more than an hour later when Ian was summoned from the waiting room. He went, as instructed, down a series of corridors. A weary Dr. Bernard met him at the entrance to his office. He put a hand gently on Ian's shoulder.

"We managed to save one of the babies."

Ian blinked in bewilderment. "*One* of the babies?"

"Your wife gave birth to twins. We had no idea. In her examinations, there was only one heartbeat. The live baby must have been lying on top of the stillborn. It doesn't happen often, but there have been isolated cases."

Ian gave an involuntary shudder. His eyes looked round and frightened, like those of a boy.

"And Catherine?"

Dr. Bernard took a deep breath. He exhaled in a sigh.

"Catherine began hemorrhaging. We were lucky to save her. But—"

"But what?" Ian asked fearfully.

"She's in a coma. She lost oxygen to the brain. I'm afraid that . . . I'm sorry."

Ian didn't even hear the doctor's words. He turned from him and walked absently to the window. He stared at his own reflection in the darkness.

It was going to be a beautiful day. Even early in the morning, the sun shone sure and strong.

Nantucket assumed a healthy glow and colors stood out with vivid clarity. There was the scent of freshness in the air. It was a perfect setting for a picture postcard. It was the stillness that was frightening.

A quiet so complete that if one listened to the lack of sounds long enough it became deafening. No screeches of birds. No rush of ocean. No children's laughter. No grown-ups whispering.

Not a soul remarking about the beautiful day.

Even the mild breeze was unnervingly still as it stroked leaves and grass with no rustling noise. . . .

Ian was in the hospital's infant viewing room when the nurse brought in his newborn child. Through eyelids weighted by lack of sleep, he became aware of activity on the other side of the plate glass that separated the freshly arrived babies from their adoring relations.

By the time Ian turned his face to the glass, Catherine's baby was already being set down into its place among the other newborns.

Ian stared woodenly through the window at his son lying in the hospital crib.

As he did so, the child's eyes opened.

The baby locked eyes with its father. Ian could not turn away. The infant looked into his mind and saw the twisted wreckage there. It looked into his heart and saw the damage. It looked into his soul and smiled a little baby grin of victory.

Part III

JULIAN

Chapter Twenty-Eight

Darkness. Impenetrable darkness. Dark as a cave. An unfathomable cavern. A warm syrup of black darkness. Nothing visible. Like the darkest depths of a mineshaft. Darkness like silk. Like marble. Shiny. Oily. Thick. Darkness unto death. No. There is movement. Soft at first, a vague stirring. Tentative. Foreign. Alien. A movement where before there was none. Hesitant. Something moves. Lightly. Like a phantom touch. Sliding. An ooze. Slow. Slippery. Like the movement of a shroud. A cover for the dead. Easy. Firm, but gentle. A movement in the deep. Climbing. Footholds. Strong, but pliant. Cover the dead with . . . the living?

New York City, 1993

Animus

In the eight years since Julian Bishop had been born, his father Ian's fortunes had prospered, but it was a very uneasy prosperity, marked with guilt and remorse.

Ian's new art gallery on Madison Avenue had blossomed into one of the most prestigious establishments of its kind, introducing a glittering array of important new creative talents. Jean de Hattan, an eccentric sculptor Ian had found on the back streets of Amsterdam, was nurtured into prominence via a one-man show that Ian sponsored in 1986. Cecile Rice from Paris scored an avant-garde knockout at the gallery the following year with her controversial paintings, which employed scraps of fetus tissue blended with charcoal. That her work had been excoriated by a prominent conservative senator from the South only added to her notoriety, and Ian made clever use of both the Pro-Choice and anti-abortion pickets who found a common ground in protesting the exhibit.

Andrew Garron, though a recluse who communicated only with Ian and exclusively through cryptic telegrams, was the toast of the art world, having been nurtured through the 1980s by an always attentive Ian. Rumors that he was a mad dope addict living in a windowless room on the Bowery only added fuel to the public's interest.

Lisa Gamble, who had been linked romantically to Garron, left Ian's employ in 1987.

Reportedly, she had traveled to Canada, settling in Toronto for a time before turning up in Vancouver. There she was discovered one morning on the floor of a rooming house, with her belly full of lye-based sink-cleaning liquid. A suicide note, scrawled on a *Three Primitives* program from the Bishop Gallery, referred to *La Bête Intérieure*, a woman's fingernails and an artist who had been driven mad by evil. The note's contents were never made public.

For his part, Ian had capitalized on the Reagan years and the attendant New York real-estate boom by selling his old gallery, purchasing outright the new gallery and buying up several more attractive properties in the area. He had also expanded downtown, opening a gallery on West Broadway in Soho and another in the rapidly burgeoning pier area of Tribeca. By the close of the '80s, he was regarded as one of the wealthiest and most successful entrepreneurs in the field and was already eyeing Europe and South America for future gallery expansion.

Ian also had invested in several Middle Eastern oil concerns, which would later prosper in the wake of the Gulf War. On a more secretive level, he had dabbled in arms sales and was a frequent visitor to Saudi Arabia and Syria.

As for Julian, he was a third grader at the Kane School, a private academy for boys near Sutton Place. An exceptionally quiet child—some would even say withdrawn—he was a straight A student who had shown an early interest in biology, model airplanes, the flute, the New York Rangers hockey team, and the poetry of Baudelaire.

Julian was not permitted to visit the Hart Clinic on Gramercy Park, where his mother Catherine remained in the coma into which she had plunged eight years earlier, on the night of his birth.

Julian was a slight child, narrow shouldered with a slim torso balanced on slender legs. His arms were long and spindly, his wrists bony, his fingers thin and delicate. Yet for all his lack of muscle, sinew and fat, there was an undeniable strength to the eight year old that no one who came in contact with him could fail to notice.

Julian's hair, kept close-cropped almost in a crew at his own insistence, was reddish and bristly. His face described a perfect oval, with a high forehead and smooth sloping cheeks curved elegantly to form a chin that was steadfast and noble. Above, a cherub's mouth, soft, almost sensuous, and a long, freckled, aquiline nose.

Then there were his eyes.

To say that they were otherworldly would suggest an acquaintance with planets whose inhabitants boasted eyes of cobalt blue, enormously large pupils—ringing irises of black like the darkest coal from the darkest pit of the universe. All of this riding silently in seas of purest milk white, capped by black velvet lashes that shimmered in their length like cobwebs.

Otherworldly—but from no planet that could be found in a universe of stars.

Otherworldly—from a deeper, more impenetrable galaxy within.

Julian had Bobo's eyes.

Chapter Twenty-nine

It was Julian's birthday. Eight years on this earth, he told himself.

Julian sat on the floor of his bedroom in the Bishops' New York apartment. The room was the same one Catherine had used as a studio when she was well. The room where she had painted likenesses of Bobo.

The room looked quite different. Gone were the art supplies and paintings, replaced by the toys, model airplanes, and sports equipment of a growing boy.

The old-world charm of Catherine's studio had given way to a high-tech gloss much more in keeping with Ian Bishop's design for the entire apartment. Track lighting. Chrome. Steel. Fiber-intensive carpeting. Black shades covered the floor-to-ceiling windows.

Julian was dressed in a stylish corduroy suit from Savile Row. He was playing the flute with an accomplished air. His long fingers moved nimbly over the holes, summoning up the melody that Catherine, as a child, used to play, sitting on the front porch of her house.

It was a melody Catherine had loved. And Julian loved it as well.

The bedroom door opened softly. Ian came in.

Ian looked much the same as he had eight years earlier, only more successful. He sported a mustache that was bushy but meticulously well-groomed. His body was perhaps a few pounds heavier, but the added weight gave him extra presence. He stood in the bedroom doorway, watching his son, listening to him play the odd melody so effortlessly. Ian looked proud.

Almost at the end of the refrain, Julian's eyes blinked. He turned his head slightly, meeting his father's gaze. He continued playing.

When he had finished the piece, Ian beckoned him toward the door. Julian stood.

"Come on into the living room, son," Ian urged. "See what we've done for your party."

Ian put an arm around Julian's shoulders. The boy said nothing.

"I haven't done this since my senior prom," Laura Spinoza said, stepping down off the ladder on which she had been standing while hanging the last of the birthday decorations.

The living room drapes were open, revealing a panoramic view of New York. Crepe paper and balloons were everywhere. A large bridge table had been set up in a corner of the room, with party favors, paper plates and presents. A "Happy Birthday, Julian" sign covered an entire wall.

Michael Spinoza nudged his wife ironically as he spied Julian coming down the hall from the bedroom.

"There he is. Happy Birthday, Julian."

Julian, walking stiffly a step behind his father, surveyed the room, but said nothing.

"Aren't you the handsome young man?" Mrs. Roberts called out in her raspy voice.

Julian glanced over at the old housekeeper. He smiled but made no reply.

"My, my," Laura said, just loud enough for her husband to hear.

Julian walked over to the bridge table. His eyes took in the brightly wrapped presents. He examined one of the envelopes and frowned.

"Beth spelled my name wrong. You spell Julian with the letter a, not the letter e."

No one seemed to notice Julian's complaint. The boy walked over to the window and looked out.

"It's starting to rain." His voice was cold, lifeless as the spray of drops on the glass.

"Probably just a shower," Laura suggested. "Maybe it'll clear up later."

Julian said nothing. He appeared to be viewing the rain with a certain satisfaction.

Ian was looking around the room rather impatiently. "Where's Beth?"

"In the kitchen," Michael replied.

Ian wandered off toward the kitchen. Laura looked at the indifferent Julian and winked at her husband.

"Looks thrilled to death, doesn't he?" she whispered.

The Bishop kitchen was unchanged from before, save for new curtains and wallpaper. Beth Wellman, a beautiful young woman, was standing at the counter. Blonde, healthy, midwestern, she exuded strength and confidence. But her movements were tempered by a soft, feminine sexuality.

Beth was arranging bite-size sandwiches on an oversize silver platter. She hummed a Lyle Lovett song in a slightly off-key fashion.

Ian appeared in the kitchen. He kissed Beth playfully on the back of the neck as if he owned it. Beth turned and kissed him lingeringly on the mouth.

"I thought you were Mrs. Roberts."

"Thanks very much," Ian said. "You made a big hit with the decorations. Julian loves them."

Beth moved back a little from his tongue. "Really? How can you tell?"

"He's my son. I know when he's happy."

"How's your hand? Steady?"

Ian held out his hand. "Like a rock."

Beth handed him a tube of icing. She pointed to a birthday cake on the kitchen counter. Ian began to squeeze out "Happy Birthday, Julian" on the top of the cake. From the other room came the sound of a doorbell, followed almost immediately by assorted greetings and the cries of excited children.

"The Mongol hordes are arriving," Ian noted, squeezing blue letters out of the tube.

"I hope they like peanut butter and jelly."

Ian ran his tongue along his lips. He smiled across at Beth. "Are you staying over?"

"I might be persuaded."

Ian stroked her hair. He kissed her hard on the mouth. A small boy appeared in the kitchen doorway.

"I gotta go to the bathroom," the boy announced.

Mrs. Roberts ducked her head in. Quickly, she led the boy off down the hall. Beth grinned. Ian finished decorating the cake. Beth looked over his shoulder and admired the lettering. She noticed the spelling of Julian's name.

"A-N, huh?" she said, almost to herself.

"Do you think there's a future for me in the catering business?" Ian asked.

"Very artistic."

Beth placed the birthday cake on a tray and began filling paper cups with lemonade.

"Did you tell Julian about his grandfather?" she asked.

Julian was suddenly standing in the doorway.

"What about my grandfather?" The boy's tone was matter-of-fact, but hard as nails.

Surprised, Ian and Beth turned. Julian leaned against the doorjamb, waiting for his father to speak.

"We have a surprise for you, son. You've heard us speak of Grandfather Bellamy—the one who lives in Switzerland. Well, he's in New York on a business trip and he's coming here this afternoon for your birthday. Julian, this is an extra-special occasion. You're going to meet your grandfather."

Beth stepped forward. "Isn't that exciting? After all this time."

Julian's eyes brightened. He smiled enigmatically.

"Yes. After all this time."

Chapter Thirty

Jason Bellamy sat in the back seat of the limousine as it cruised through midtown traffic. The left side of his face was smooth and unscarred. The right side, as was Jason Bellamy's custom, was turned away from view, pressed against the nearest surface. In this case, the smooth leather of the automobile's interior.

Now in his mid-sixties, Jason was still a firm-jawed, determined-looking man with a striking intensity. As the limousine turned onto a side street, he stared ahead resolutely. It had begun to rain.

The party was well under way. In the living room of the Bishop apartment, a dozen children were romping about, while parents and governesses mingled with one another. The bridge table and surrounding area were strewn with opened birthday presents, wrapping paper and ribbons. Paper plates and cups were in abundance. Julian sat alone in the corner, smiling but aloof, taking it all in.

Drew, a pretty little girl with short, dark hair and sparkling blue eyes, approached Julian. She motioned toward a game of Pin the Tail on the Donkey.

"Come on, Julian, play with us."

Julian looked at her gently. "Maybe later." His voice came from far away.

In another corner of the living room, Michael and Laura were sipping drinks. Laura nodded toward Julian.

"Look at him," she whispered, so as not to be overheard by Ian and Beth who were engaged in a lively conversation on the couch. "Julian is like the pope. He's given us an audience. We're lucky to be in the same room."

Michael chuckled. "Laura, he's eight years old. He's a little shy, that's all."

"He's not shy. He thinks he's better than all of us."

"Don't be silly."

Michael wandered over toward Julian's corner of the room. He put his arm around the boy's shoulders.

"Are you having a good time, Julian?"

"Yes. Are you?"

"Laura and I are having a wonderful time. I

just saw you sitting by yourself over here."

"My grandfather's coming from Switzerland."

Jason Bellamy got off the elevator. He walked down the corridor toward the Bishop apartment. He rang the bell. The door was opened by Mrs. Roberts.

Behind the old housekeeper was Julian. The eight year old's eyes grew large as he stared knowingly at Jason Bellamy.

At Jason Bellamy's face.

From the eye down to the jawline, Jason's right cheek was horribly scarred, ravaged by the cuts he inflicted with the razor 25 years before.

Julian continued to stare at his grandfather's mutilated visage. The expression on the boy's face was one of satisfaction. Even vindication.

Julian walked purposefully across the room and extended his hand to Mr. Bellamy.

"Hello, Grandfather. I've been waiting for you."

It was some time later that Julian was called on to blow out the birthday candles. His eight-year-old features danced crazily in the light from the blazing wicks.

As Julian gathered in his breath, Mrs. Roberts prompted him from behind.

"Don't forget to make a wish, Julian."

Julian's mouth wrinkled in a brief smile.

Then he stared intently across the table at Mr. Bellamy. The boy's smile widened. For a split second, he appeared almost angelic.

Like an angel of death. . . .

Jason Bellamy shifted uncomfortably under the boy's gaze. He turned his aged eyes away, but he could still feel the piercing look the child was giving him. Fierce determination blazed on Julian's face as the boy blew out the candles.

Jason Bellamy shivered. It was as though an icy wind had blown through the chambers of his heart.

Half an hour later, the children had begun to grow restless. Their polite chatter had turned to a loud clamor. Remnants of birthday cake lay on paper plates. Mrs. Roberts had already begun clearing away the debris. Julian, for the moment, was nowhere to be seen.

"It's near the whaling museum," Beth said. "It's not far from where the ferry comes in."

Beside her on the sofa, Jason Bellamy rubbed his chin thoughtfully. "I haven't been on Nantucket for ages. I think I know where you mean."

"Beth's only had the shop for two years," Ian explained. He was on the other side of Beth, his left arm protectively draped around her shoulders.

"Ian saw one of my scrimshaw bracelets in the window. He came in to price it and that's how we met."

Ian held up his hand. On his wrist was a seashell bracelet inlayed on silver.

"A hundred and fifty dollars. I think she sold it below cost just to keep me around."

Ian extended his hand for Jason Bellamy's inspection. The older man studied the bracelet admiringly, then smiled across at Beth.

"You're very talented. My daughter was an artist too."

"I know. I saw one of her dolls in a shop on Main Street. The owner wouldn't part with it. It was quite fascinating, almost lifelike."

"Catherine and her dolls," Ian said, almost to himself. "She had quite an imagination."

Jason nodded thoughtfully, his mind seemingly back in the long ago past.

"Yes, even as a child," he sighed.

"I keep asking Ian to show me some of her work," Beth said.

"It's at the summer house. It's all stored away. I'll show it to you sometime."

Jason Bellamy leaned forward. He thought he saw something. Was it Julian and a tomboyish little girl slipping out onto the terrace?

"Tell me about Zurich," Beth said. "I hear it's absolutely lovely."

Jason looked again. The door to the terrace had closed. Perhaps he had imagined the two children going out there.

"I went to Zurich originally for plastic surgery," Jason heard himself saying. "After I got out of the clinic, I spent some time in the mountains recuperating. Switzerland worked its magic on me. It has a certain life-giving charm. Before I knew it, I was living there."

Unnoticed by the three of them, but clearly visible through the glass of the nearby window, Julian had enticed the little girl onto the narrow ledge of the terrace. He was pointing upward, motioning for the child to lean back in order to see what he was pointing at.

The little girl leaned back, swaying dangerously on the narrow ledge, several floors over the street.

"I have some money in a Swiss bank account," Ian boasted. "Maybe you could look in on it for me."

"Aren't you the clever one?" Beth laughed. "You never told me about—"

"Oh, my God!" Jason jumped to his feet and raced out toward the terrace. Beth and Ian, looking confused, ran after him. The old man reached the entrance to the narrow cement terrace first.

Julian was waiting for him.

As Jason skidded to a stop, Julian looked up at him with wide-eyed innocence. He smiled.

Behind Julian, the tomboy girl was oblivious as she teetered high above the Manhattan street. Her head bobbed back and forth. She was still trying to spy what Julian had been pointing at, even as her slender legs threatened to buckle.

With surprising agility, Jason Bellamy sprang

past Julian and across the terrace. He scooped the bewildered young girl into his sturdy arms. Ian and Beth were just arriving in the doorway.

"I just wanted to see the pigeons," the girl exclaimed. "Julian said there was a nest up there."

Julian had rushed to his father and was embracing him.

"She wasn't going to fall. I was holding her."

Jason tried to stare the boy down. "You were nowhere near her."

"I was holding her," Julian repeated defiantly.

"Jesus," Jason Bellamy muttered, "if I hadn't grabbed her. . . ."

"Let's go inside, son," Ian suggested. "You shouldn't be playing on the terrace."

"Playing?" Jason sputtered in disbelief.

Ian led Julian inside.

"Nothing was going to happen, Daddy," the boy insisted.

Ian hugged him. "I know."

Jason followed them, taking the little girl's hand. "I just wanted to see the pigeons," she repeated.

The terrace door closed.

Beth found herself alone on the terrace. She stepped back toward the ledge and looked up. The ledges above were empty. There were no signs that birds had ever nested there.

Chapter Thirty-One

Nearly midnight, the same night.

The Bishop living room was lit only by a small night lamp. The birthday decorations and remnants of the party had been removed, restoring the room to its normal pristine state.

Down the hallway, the door to Mrs. Roberts's room was shut for the night. Behind it, under her mounds of blankets, the housekeeper slept the sleep of the proper, her aged ears not sensitive enough to pick out the faint sound that drifted quietly through the Bishop home.

The faint sound of a flute. Coming from farther down the hallway.

In the Bishop guest room, a dim light burned. The room was small and comfortable, with a single bed. The covers were turned back. A book was on the night table, unread that night.

Restless and unable to sleep, Jason Bellamy stood in front of the window. He looked out on the void of New York at night. The moonlight gave his scarred face a haunted severity.

The strains of the flute grew slightly louder. Jason stared at his reflection in the glass, as though remembering something from distant history.

Putting a robe on over his pajamas, he moved woodenly toward the door.

Outside, in the corridor, the old man walked slowly toward a closed door. As he advanced, the flute music grew louder in his ears. He reached the door. From behind it, the flute was being played. He paused. His hand went to the doorknob.

Jason was listening more carefully. He looked startled at what he heard. A frame from his past had slipped eerily into the movie of his life.

The old man listened for another moment outside Julian Bishop's room, then continued on down the hallway.

The only light in the kitchen came from the dim bulb over the stove. Ian, also in pajamas and robe, was spreading mustard on a hero sandwich he had just concocted. He looked up as Jason came into the room. Ian smiled. It was almost as though he were expecting him. He pointed to the overstuffed sandwich with a degree of pride.

"Care to join me? I've got salami and American cheese and some hot peppers. Beth would kill me."

"No. No, thanks," Jason murmured. He moved forlornly, like a sleepwalker.

"There's some roast beef in the fridge."

"Nothing for me."

"You want a beer?"

Jason sat down wearily in a rocking chair. "I just heard something very peculiar. Julian was playing a melody on the flute that Catherine used to play as a child."

Jason hummed the melody. Ian nodded.

"I know that song," Ian said. "Julian plays it all the time. He told me that he made it up."

Jason looked puzzled. "That's impossible. Catherine made it up."

"Catherine?"

"Many years ago."

"Catherine's been in a coma since. . . ."

"I know."

"Then how would Julian know it?"

Jason shook his head. "I don't know."

In the doorway, unseen by the two men, stood Julian, the flute in his hand. His face was a portrait of determination and cunning.

"It's a simple enough melody," Ian noted, adopting his pedantic air. "What is it? Five notes? It probably just sounds similar."

"No. It's the same," Jason said quietly.

"I didn't know Catherine played the flute."

"Catherine drove me to distraction playing that flute. I finally had to take it away from her."

"Do you think that was wise? You might have nipped a musical genius in the bud."

Jason sighed. His face looked old and ravaged for death. "I doubt that. She didn't really have an ear for melody."

From the shadows of the doorway, Julian eyed the old man with contempt.

"I'm surprised Catherine never mentioned the flute," Ian said. "She told me a great deal about her childhood." He paused. "She even told me about Bobo."

"Bobo?"

"Her imaginary playmate."

Jason squinted into the darkness, remembering. "Oh, yes, Bobo. She talked about him all the time until she was eight years old."

"What happened then?"

"That's when I had my accident. She never brought him up after that. It's odd that she would tell you about him. It was all such a long time ago."

"She mentioned it in passing." Ian's tone was smug. "She just laughed it off as a childhood fantasy."

Jason nodded. "That's all it ever was."

In the doorway, Julian's cold look of hatred flared at both the men.

Chapter Thirty-Two

The next morning. Eight o'clock. A barge made its way dreamily down the river. The sun was low in the sky, but promised a beautiful day.

Outside the Bishop apartment building, there was the usual prework flurry. Men and women were exiting the lobby hurriedly. Blowing his whistle, the uniformed doorman hailed cabs.

Ian and Beth emerged from the building. Beth carried an overnight bag. Ian saw her into a taxi, kissed her good-bye, then flagged down a separate cab for himself.

Upstairs in the Bishop apartment, Jason Bellamy was already awake. Dressed in a bathrobe, he stood before the bathroom mirror. The glass reflected the high-ceilinged room's elegant space, its luxurious marble fixtures.

Jason took an electric razor from his shaving kit.

He plugged the razor's cord into the wall socket and began to shave.

Jason adjusted the mirror. He saw something in its glass motion.

Julian was in the doorway.

Already dressed for school in a dark blue suit, the boy was studying him. Jason was reminded of the way a child might look at a beetle under a microscope in the sun.

"Good morning, Julian," Jason said. He was trying to be nonchalant, but the greeting rasped in his throat.

Julian made no reply.

"You're up early, aren't you?"

Again, no answer.

Jason met the boy's eyes in the mirror. An insolent smile lit the boy's lips.

"How did you hurt your face?"

Jason felt himself grow tense. "It was an accident."

Julian's eyes grew dark. "You cut yourself, didn't you? You were shaving."

"It was an accident."

"You did it with a razor blade." The eight year old pointed to the electric shaver. "Is that why you use one of those now?"

Jason turned around. He eyed the boy with disapproval.

"Shouldn't you be getting ready for school?"

Again, the insolent smile dimpled the corners of the child's mouth.

"My mother was there. She saw you do it. You made her cry that day."

Jason was getting nervous. He turned back to the mirror. Hoping to avoid the boy's eyes. That smile.

"How do you know that?" Jason heard himself asking.

"She had a present for you," Julian went on. "A picture. You didn't want to look."

The boy took a folded piece of paper from the inside pocket of his dark jacket.

"Would you like to see it now?"

Julian unfolded the paper. Jason glanced at the picture. His eyes glazed over.

It was the same drawing of Jason that Catherine had done 25 years earlier.

Julian watched calmly from the doorway. He knew that the strength was in him. Jason's shoulders were slumping. The weakness was taking over.

Jason slipped into a trancelike state. He stared at the electric razor still buzzing in his hand. Then, methodically, he put it down on the marble sink. Next to it was Ian's shaving kit, with the initials IPB embossed in gold lettering on the top.

Jason unfastened the kit and took out Ian's manual razor. He raised it to his face as though to shave.

Julian watched curiously from the doorway.

Jason's hand paused. He looked at the shaving device, then slowly removed the single-edged blade.

Just then, Julian spoke. His voice was a hiss, an eerie whisper.

"Catherine loved you. You should never have hurt her."

Serenely, watching himself in the bathroom mirror, Jason proceeded to slit his throat from ear to ear. Gushers of blood shot out in all directions, bathing the walls and fixtures with a vivid crimson.

The razor blade slipped from Jason's hand and clattered into the sink. In agony, the old man crashed to the ground, blood pouring from his severed jugular vein.

Julian smiled through his intense curiosity.

Next to the bathroom wall was an antique iron doorstop, embedded in the tile. It was pointed, about two inches in height, and it made a deep incision in Jason's head as he landed smack upon it—a lasting impression.

Jason's body lay twitching for a moment, then was still. Covered in the blood that had splashed his way, Julian smiled in final satisfaction from the doorway.

He folded up Catherine's drawing with reverence and returned it to the pocket of his coat.

A noise from the hallway outside made Julian turn slowly. An alarmed Mrs. Roberts had stopped in her tracks in the corridor. Wrapped in her bathrobe, she took in the gruesome scene on the bloody bathroom floor.

Jason Bellamy was dead. The housekeeper's wise old eyes told her that much. He was dead in a pool of his own blood. Julian was facing her. He showed no reaction, save for a vacant stare.

214

Chapter Thirty-Three

Three days later, Ian Bishop and Mrs. Roberts stood solemnly on the tarmac at JFK Airport as Jason Bellamy's coffin was loaded onto a plane bound for Switzerland.

In the limousine returning to Manhattan, Ian stared glumly out the window.

"That's nice. A man comes all the way from Switzerland to commit suicide in my bathroom."

Mrs. Roberts didn't answer. She stared out the opposite window, still trying to gather her thoughts together.

"Right in front of my son," Ian continued. "That's a heavy thing for Julian to go through. He's only eight years old. I just hope this won't have some terrible effect on him."

"He didn't seem very upset," the housekeeper noted quietly.

"I beg your pardon."

"The boy didn't react. He showed absolutely no response. Poor Mr. Bellamy was lying there dead and Julian just looked at him. He still hasn't shown any emotion."

Ian squinted at the old lady. "Are you suggesting Julian is in some kind of shock?"

"He doesn't seem to be. He went to school today. He acts as if nothing happened."

"That's what I mean. He's probably blocking the entire thing out."

"Perhaps." Mrs. Roberts didn't sound convinced.

"What else could it be? Julian's a sensitive child. If he didn't react, he must be holding it all in."

Mrs. Roberts shifted her weight against the seat cushion. She continued looking out the window as Queens gave way to Manhattan.

Later that day, Ian took time off from his gallery duties to limo up to Julian's private school, an imposing, very traditional edifice on a side street in the 80s, just off Park Avenue.

A bell rang. Children began pouring out of the building. Julian was the last one out, descending the front steps with a poise and assurance belying his eight years. Ian was waiting for him on the sidewalk.

"Daddy!"

Ian put an arm around the boy's shoulders in a friendly fashion. "I thought I'd surprise you. It's a nice day. Would you like to walk home?"

Julian nodded. Ian took the boy's hand and the two of them started toward nearby Central Park.

When they were opposite Cleopatra's Needle, just behind the Metropolitan Museum, Ian studied his son.

"How do you feel? Are you all right?"

"I'm fine. No homework tonight."

"I mean about the other day. What happened to your grandfather."

"I'm okay. Daddy, can we watch the *Terminator* video?"

"After dinner." Ian paused. "Your grandfather was a very sick man. Do you understand that?"

"I guess so."

"He was disturbed."

"I know. His blood went all over the bathroom tiles. You can still see the stains."

Ian looked at the boy, more concerned than ever.

"I had a talk with Julian yesterday. He's very troubled about what happened."

Ian was seated in the dining room of the Spinoza apartment the following evening. On either side of him in the small comfortable room distinguished by lovely Queen Anne furnishings were Michael and Laura. Low in the background, a recording of a Bach harpsichord piece was playing.

"I'm taking Julian up to Nantucket for the rest of the school year," Ian said grandly. "A change of scenery will be good for both of us."

"What about the galleries?" Laura asked.

"My assistant can handle things. I'm a phone call away."

"The boy's keeping it all in," Michael said. "Am I right?"

Ian nodded. "He's trying to be a little man about it. A little tough guy. He doesn't want to let on that he's shook up."

"Poor little fella. I'd be shook up too."

Laura's eyes bounced off her husband. "What does Julian say? Has he talked to you at all about the suicide?"

"That's just it," Ian replied. "He doesn't say anything. Mrs. Roberts noticed it too. It's as if nothing happened. It wouldn't surprise me if he's in some mild form of shock."

"Do you think the boy needs to see a doctor?" Michael wondered.

Ian drew back slightly. "You mean a shrink? Don't tell me—Janet Parker."

"She's very good," Michael said cautiously. "I know the two of you didn't see eye to eye."

"That's putting it mildly."

"She knew Catherine," Michael went on. "She knows the family background. Maybe she can help."

218

Ian gave him a cold stare. "She didn't help Catherine."

Laura leaned forward, suddenly angry. "That's not true. Catherine was afraid of having a baby. Dr. Parker helped her overcome that fear."

"It's just a suggestion, Ian. Give it some thought."

Ian put down his knife and fork. "I will, but I think Nantucket is the answer."

Michael smiled supportively. Laura looked dubious.

Chapter Thirty-Four

The following Saturday, around noon, Mrs.
Roberts was in the kitchen preparing soup
and a health salad for two. On the counter
in front of her was a tiny, battery-operated
television. As she chopped vegetables for the
salad, Mrs. Roberts chuckled at the antics of
two wrestlers, who were challenging each other
to a future bout at the top of their lungs.

The housekeeper added dressing to the salad
and spooned out two portions onto plates. She
went out into the hallway in search of Julian.

His bedroom door looked closed.

As Mrs. Roberts proceeded down the corridor, the sound of the TV died out and was
replaced by a familiar melody on the flute coming from Julian's room.

Animus

Coming closer, the housekeeper noticed that the door to the bedroom was slightly ajar. She paused before it. She leaned forward. She peeked inside.

Sitting cross-legged on the floor was Julian. He was playing the flute in front of a silver-framed photograph of his mother. As Mrs. Roberts watched, Julian finished the tune. He put down the instrument and touched the photograph lovingly. He spoke to the picture.

"You weren't supposed to die, Catherine. I'd have taken care of you. It was Ian's fault. He hurt you inside. You weren't supposed to die."

Suddenly, Julian turned.

He caught sight of the aged housekeeper standing in the doorway. He smiled at her with an unearthly gleam in his little boy eyes.

"Would you like to tell me what that was all about? Where did you get that picture and why were you talking to it?"

It was a few minutes later. Julian was seated at the kitchen table, picking at his salad. Mrs. Roberts felt decidedly more comfortable now that the two of them were back in the room she considered her domain. She stirred the soup on the stove.

"It was just a game," Julian mumbled.

"It didn't look like a game. And since when do you call your mother by her first name?"

"I was only playing."

"And that stuff about your father gave me the creeps just listening to it."

Mrs. Roberts moved over to the counter. She began preparing herself a health drink consisting of carrot juice, two raw eggs and crushed ice, all mixed together in a blender.

" 'You weren't supposed to die, Catherine.' What does that mean? Your mother's not dead. Technically, that is. And even if she were, the good Lord takes each of us when our time comes. You know that, Julian."

The boy watched as Mrs. Roberts switched on the blender. After a few seconds, she clicked it off and poured the drink into a large glass. She drained the glass in a single gulp. Julian looked very interested.

"You swallowed the ice too."

Mrs. Roberts nodded. "Yes, if you blend the ice chips fine enough, you don't even feel them going down."

"Oh."

Julian regarded the blender thoughtfully. His eyes widened. A smile tugged at his lips.

Ian decided to have a talk with his son. Julian was sitting on his bed in his pajamas and robe, engrossed in drawing on a sketch pad.

Julian glanced up when Ian entered. Ian shut the door behind him and sat down on the bed.

"I think we need to talk. Man to man."

Julian nodded knowingly. "Mrs. Roberts told you."

"She's concerned about you, little man. So am I."

222

"I told her I was just playing."

"You were talking to a picture of your mother. You called her Catherine."

"No, I didn't. She's lying."

"You talked about her dying. You know that's not true."

"She's alive. I know that."

"You said I hurt her."

"I never said that." The boy rubbed his small fists into his eyes.

"You said that Catherine died because of me. That it was my fault."

Julian burst into tears. "No, Daddy, no! It's not true. She's lying!"

In a matter of seconds, the boy was weeping hysterically. Ian, a bit alarmed, tried to comfort him. Holding him, he rocked the boy back and forth in his arms. A few minutes went by and Julian seemed to calm down.

"I was talking to the picture," the child said slowly, enunciating each word. "But I never said those things. Mrs. Roberts made them up. Do you believe me?"

Ian tucked him into bed and kissed him on the forehead.

"I'll see you in the morning."

"Night, Daddy."

Ian picked up the sketch pad from the bed. He crossed the room and turned out the light. He opened the door and the light from the hallway shone on the sketch pad. Absently, Ian glanced at the pad as he put it on the boy's dresser.

The sketch was a remarkable likeness of Catherine. Underneath, in Julian's childish scrawl: "I love you, Catherine."

In the living room, Ian looked up an old telephone number. He dialed it. A familiar voice answered. Ian looked startled as he stared out the window at the Manhattan skyline, half shrouded in night.

"I was all set to leave a message," Ian said gruffly. "I didn't think you'd be in."

"Who is this?"

"Ian Bishop."

There was a pause on the other end of the line. The woman's voice betrayed curiosity.

"Yes, Catherine's husband. How are you, Mr. Bishop?"

Down the hall, in the bedroom Ian had just left, Julian was under the covers, seemingly asleep. Suddenly, his eyes shot open.

Julian sat up slowly in bed.

For a moment, he appeared to be concentrating. Getting his bearings. He looked around the room vaguely. Then his gaze focused on a phone on the desk near the window.

Quietly, Julian got out of bed. He went over to the phone. With a practiced stealth, he lifted the receiver and put it to his ear. He listened to the conversation his father was having with a woman, a stranger.

"Well, then. . . ."

"I don't usually make house calls, Mr. Bishop."

"He's only eight years old. He's been through a very shocking experience. I'd like you to see him, but I'd like it to be as informal as possible. If you could come by the apartment, you could be with him in a comfortable setting."

"I'm free Monday afternoon. From four to six."

"That's fine, Dr. Parker. I'll expect you then."

Julian gently replaced the receiver. He stared out the window malevolently.

Dr. Parker. Dr. Parker. . . .

Chapter Thirty-Five

Dr. Janet Parker's life had not changed substantially since that day eight years earlier when Ian had hung up on her, prior to spiriting Catherine off to Nantucket. Janet was 46 years old, still unmarried, still chic and attractive, still working out of her warm, friendly office on West End Avenue. She had added to her collection of David Hockney prints and complemented them with a vigorously offensive Francis Bacon reproduction, which, given its depiction of the human spirit, Janet kept in the private wing of her office. No use stirring up the clients with difficult images when they came to her with a longing for serenity.

"It's a remarkable likeness. Did he do it from a photo?"

It was Monday afternoon. Ian and Janet were sitting in the Bishop living room having tea. Janet was inspecting the sketch of Catherine that Julian drew.

"Yes, of course," Ian replied. "Julian's never been to see Catherine. He doesn't even know where she is."

"But he knows she's alive?"

"He knows that she had an accident. The particulars are not known to him. The circumstances of her present conditions are unavailable to him."

Dr. Parker couldn't help noticing that Ian spoke like a computer on this matter. She smiled slightly. Oh, well, he had always had it in him. Catherine's absence had merely intensified that characteristic.

Ian handed her a photograph of Catherine. Janet compared it to the sketch.

"He's drawn a necklace," Janet pointed out. "That's not in the photo. Looks like little doll figures."

Ian appeared surprised. He took a closer look at the sketch.

"That's odd," Ian mused. "Catherine had a necklace like that. Laura gave it to her. But I don't remember her ever wearing it. In fact, I haven't seen it for years. I thought it was packed away with the rest of Catherine's things in Nantucket."

"He's a good little artist."

"Yes, he got that from Catherine. You know,

I'm going to look for that necklace when I get up there."

"How soon are you leaving?"

"Next week sometime. I have to clear it with Julian's school. They're very regimented over there. Not that I'm complaining. Order does the boy good."

"How's he doing in school?"

"Straight A's." Ian sighed gruffly. "There's no problem there. He got a hundred on a test on Friday."

The front door opened. Julian came in, carrying his schoolbooks. Seeing Janet, he allowed a slight smile. "Hello."

"This is Janet Parker," Ian said. "She's an old friend of mine. My son, Julian."

Julian extended his hand. Janet shook it. His fingers felt like icicles.

"Janet and I haven't seen each other for eight years."

Julian perked up. "Oh? Did you know my mother?"

"Yes, I did," Janet smiled. "She was a lovely woman."

Ian led his son to the couch. "Julian, I want you to sit down for a few minutes. Janet wants to talk to you. I have a few phone calls to make. I'll be in the next room if you need me."

Ian patted the boy on the head affectionately, then left. Julian took off his coat and sat down. He looked over at Dr. Parker warily.

"You're a doctor."

Janet was impressed. "Yes, I'm a psychologist. Do you know what that is?"

"Yes. Are you here because of my grandfather?"

Janet hesitated. She wasn't sure exactly how much the boy knew. "Yes. How do you feel about that?"

Julian shrugged. "He wasn't very nice."

"You only met him once."

"He wasn't very nice to my mother."

"Oh?"

"She used to have bad dreams about him."

"How do you know that?"

Julian leaned forward. "It's true, isn't it?"

Janet paused. Maybe if she changed the subject.

"I was admiring your drawing. You think a lot about your mother, don't you?"

"She died when I was born."

"Is that what you think?"

"She stopped being here. Something happened. She went away. She wasn't the same."

"And you call that dying?"

"It started when I was born. Something stopped. Something started."

Janet considered his remarks. Her eyes caught Julian's. "But you talk to her?"

"Yes." The boy's voice was soft, like a breeze wafting in the late afternoon air.

"What do you say?"

Julian kept his gaze up. "Things. I pretend."

"Do you pretend that she's alive?"

The boy looked away. He played with his icicle fingers. Then he looked back up. "Yes."

"Do you pretend that she talks to you?"

"She doesn't have to."

Janet looked at the boy curiously. She let his eyes follow hers down to the sketch.

"You wrote on the drawing: 'I love you, Catherine.'"

"Right."

"But you never met her."

"Yes, I did. She's my mother. I lived inside her."

Afterward, Janet Parker conferred with Ian over coffee at the kitchen table. The door was closed.

"I don't think you should take Julian to Nantucket," the doctor began. "There's something wrong. He seems unstable. I'd like him to start regular sessions in my office."

Ian waved his hand dismissively. "Look, I just got off the phone with his principal. He's going to Nantucket. I think once he's out of this apartment, he'll forget about what happened to his grandfather."

"I'm not so sure about that," Janet said quietly. "I think Mr. Bellamy's suicide is only part of the problem."

"What do you mean?"

"I don't know. There's something strange about the way Julian relates. It has to do with his mother."

"That's absurd." Ian was growing angry now. "Julian has no problem relating. He's a bright, sensitive child. Put him on the beach at Nantucket and he'll be fine."

"I doubt that. I don't believe that's the answer."

"I think we had this conversation before, Dr. Parker. Eight years ago. I took Catherine to Nantucket. Now I'm taking Julian to Nantucket. That's final. All right?"

Janet eyed Ian for a moment. She stirred her coffee pensively. "Mr. Bishop, did you ever tell Julian about Catherine's dream?"

Ian looked puzzled. "Her dream?"

"The nightmare about her father."

"No. Of course not."

"I didn't think so."

Chapter Thirty-Six

Nantucket never changed. Even though the islanders—the year-rounders, as some called them—complained, generation after generation, about the inroads being made on their ocean hideaway by the dreaded mainlanders, Nantucket remained the same enchanted isle it had always been. Especially in springtime.

In spring, the first lukewarm breezes crept in off the water, promising the impossible—that the frigid cold that had enveloped the island since the previous October would soon give way to lovely days of warmth and renewal.

Spring was still lagging behind the mainland by a good three weeks as Julian walked along the Nantucket beach, his young face turned toward the ocean on which several early sailboats bobbed. Julian played the flute as he went along, squinting into the afternoon sun, fingering notes that seemed to come to him from another source—filtered through his fingers to the instrument itself.

It was a familiar melody—one as old as Good and Evil.

Julian left the beach, starting up the wooded path in the direction of the Bellamy house. In the kitchen of that house, Mrs. Roberts was just putting the lunch plates into the dishwasher. The phone rang.

"Bishop residence," the housekeeper answered.

Beth Wellman's scrimshaw shop was a small, brightly painted establishment near the Nantucket ferry dock. Its windows, on either side of a handsome oak door, displayed a variety of scrimshaw pieces, ranging from inexpensive earrings and cuff links to extravagantly priced ship models and picture frames. Over the door was a cheerful sign that said simply: *Beth's Nook*.

In the glass of the window was another sign that read: *Will Return in One Hour*.

Inside the shop, Ian's voice boomed out from the back room.

"I'm at the gas station, Mrs. Roberts. There's something wrong with the carburetor."

Hearing Beth giggle, Ian covered the phone receiver with his hand. The double bed they lay on, nude, took up a good part of Beth's cozy living space.

"It's nothing serious, Mrs. Roberts. I'll be back later."

Ian hung up the receiver. Beth broke out laughing. "The carburetor? Why don't you tell her the truth?"

"That I'm in town for a quickie?"

Beth slapped Ian playfully across the jaw. "Uh uh. I'm not giving out quickies today."

Ian laughed. He kissed her greedily on the mouth.

Julian opened the door quietly and came in from the porch. He listened. He looked down the hall toward the kitchen. Mrs. Roberts was at the dishwasher. Taking care not to be noticed, Julian went quickly to the staircase.

The Bellamy attic was a large cluttered room with sloping walls. It was filled with cartons, trunks and discarded bits of furniture. A large spider's web glistened in the sunlight that streamed through the dusty window.

Julian came up the stairs that led into the room. He looked around for a minute with a penetrating gaze, as though trying to conjure up the whereabouts of some item.

Bird sounds drifted in from outside. After several moments, Julian walked purposefully toward a large gold trunk in the corner of the room. He knelt down in front of it.

Gently, he eased open the lid.

The trunk was filled to the brim with art books, brushes, a palette—Catherine's supplies. In the center of the trunk, wrapped carefully in soft velvet, was an object Julian recognized.

He picked it up, knowingly, and began to unfold the velvet, revealing the malevolent child doll.

Julian admired the doll, almost worshipfully.

A voice came from behind him.

"Julian."

Stunned, Julian whirled around.

"What are you doing up here?" Mrs. Roberts asked from the top of the stairs.

Julian didn't answer. His fingers went to the doll's chest. Still around its neck was the necklace, the gift from Laura Spinoza years before. In the breast pocket of the doll's tuxedo jacket, a small white handkerchief had been added. Embroidered on it meticulously was the single name Bobo.

Mrs. Roberts was staring. Julian's face was nearly side by side with the face of the malevolent boy doll. But what Catherine had painted years earlier had some finishing touches in her son. A wig was fixed to its head and its facial features were more pronounced.

It was a miniature, but perfect duplicate of Julian.

*   *   *

"I can't get over how much he looks like you," Mrs. Roberts said. "Your father's not going to believe it."

It was a few minutes later as Julian sat on a stool next to the kitchen counter, eating a peanut butter and jelly sandwich. Across from him on the counter was perched the malevolent boy doll. Mrs. Roberts shook her head at the resemblance.

Julian didn't reply to her observation. A slight, superior smile tugged at the corners of his mouth.

You'd be surprised.

Later, after Julian had polished off a root beer, he stood at the kitchen sink, looking through the window. With a floppy straw hat protecting her from the sun, Mrs. Roberts, on her hands and knees, was pulling weeds in the garden.

Julian turned away from the window. He looked at the doll on the counter. Their eyes met.

As though being watched and instructed, Julian took three eggs and cracked them into a bowl. He took Mrs. Roberts's blender and poured the eggs into it. He added carrot juice, then went to the refrigerator and took out a tray of small ice cubes. He dumped several ice cubes into the blender. He put the ice tray back in the refrigerator and returned to

236

the sink. He took a small drinking glass down
from the cabinet. He looked out the window
once again. Mrs. Roberts was still in the garden. He glanced back at the doll, then went
over to it. Gently, he removed the embroidered
handkerchief from the breast pocket. Returning
to the sink, he carefully wrapped the glass in
the handkerchief. With a single, swift blow, he
smashed the glass against the side of the sink.
He unwrapped the handkerchief and began to
take slivers of glass from the cloth. He put them
into the bowl of the blender, mixing them in
with the other ingredients. He set the blender
for puree and pushed the on button. He smiled
as the blender whirred and the sharp slivers of
glass were blended into Mrs. Roberts's health
drink.

Mrs. Roberts was still weeding when Julian
emerged from the house.

The boy squinted into the sun. "Mrs.
Roberts," he called out. The housekeeper
straightened her aged frame. She looked
around. "Yes," she called back vaguely.

"I have a surprise for you."

Mrs. Roberts spied the boy at last. She scurried toward the house.

Julian held the door for her. The old woman
went inside. A smile lit up her face.

On the kitchen counter was her health drink
in a glass next to the blender. Mrs. Roberts
patted Julian affectionately on the cheek.

"Aren't you a sweetheart!"

The housekeeper tasted the drink. She smiled at the boy, who was watching her attentively.

"It's perfect," Mrs. Roberts pronounced.

Julian continued to watch her. There was mounting triumph in his expression.

Mrs. Roberts drank the concoction down, chopped glass and all. She finished the drink, smacked her lips and sat down, removing her sun hat.

"That was lovely, Julian. Thank you."

The boy's grin widened. "If you blend the ice chips fine enough, you don't even feel them going down."

Mrs. Roberts put her hand to her chest. She cleared her throat. She coughed a little.

Julian's eyes met hers. "You shouldn't have spied on me," he said, his voice just above a whisper.

The housekeeper was trying to catch her breath. She moved in the chair uncomfortably.

"What?" she asked hoarsely. "What do you mean, Julian?"

"I was talking to Catherine. You were nosy. You shouldn't have said anything to Ian."

Mrs. Roberts looked confused. She was about to answer. She coughed instead.

Blood trickled from her mouth.

"Ian hurt Catherine inside," Julian continued. "He'll pay for that. You interfered, you nosy old bitch. You always interfered."

The glass was reaching Mrs. Roberts's stomach. The old woman began to writhe in pain.

She stumbled to her feet. She thrust her fingers down her throat, desperately hoping to vomit up the glass.

More blood poured from her mouth.

Julian looked on calmly.

The pain in the old housekeeper's belly was too much for her. She began to retch blood.

She pitched forward onto the kitchen floor.

Her face even with the floorboards, she looked up at Julian pleadingly.

"Julian, for God's sake. . . ."

Mrs. Roberts's mouth went slack. She quivered for a moment. Her body went limp.

She was dead.

Nonchalantly, Julian got up. He walked over to the sink. He picked up the handkerchief that contained the remainder of the glass slivers.

Julian went over to the counter and gently returned the handkerchief to the breast pocket of the malevolent boy doll. He tucked the doll under his arm and started toward the kitchen door, stepping casually over Mrs. Roberts's body.

Passing the cookie jar, Julian reached in and extracted an Oreo. He munched on it as he left the kitchen.

Once in the living room, the boy crossed quickly to the fireplace. He stirred up the logs, giving the fire more intensity.

Julian tossed the doll into the flames. It began to burn instantly. Julian jabbed it with a poker to speed things up. Soon the doll was just ashes.

The boy looked up. Perfect timing.

He could hear Ian's car, which had turned off the main road onto the backwoods thoroughfare leading to the house.

Julian smiled. He hurried to the front door, opened it and ran quickly down the steps as Ian was screeching to a halt.

"Daddy! Daddy! Something's happened to Mrs. Roberts!"

Chapter Thirty-Seven

The air had been stifling all day.

Dark bulky clouds hung in the sky like blankets, seeming to press down on the island with their humid mass. A hot sun shone through them, but was barely visible.

The promise of a cooling rain was present, but little more than a tease as afternoon wore on.

Beth's scrimshaw shop was still open, but there were no customers at the moment. Soon, the Friday afternoon rush would begin. But for the moment, there was a bit of rest time for Beth, who stood behind the counter holding a piece of official-looking paper in her hand.

At the top of the sheet of paper were the words *Office of the Coroner*. Below it was a blank for the name of the deceased. Typed in that space was the name of Evelyn Roberts, her age and birthplace. At the bottom of the page, in the space listing cause of death, was typed: "Perforated Ulcers, Internal Hemorrhaging."

"Seems cold, doesn't it?" Beth said. "A person's life ends and it's all on paper."

Across from her, his bulky frame squeezed into a wicker rocking chair, Ian grunted.

Beth handed the document back to Ian. He folded it in half and stuck it in his pocket.

"How's Julian taking it?" Beth asked.

"Pretty hard," Ian sighed. "He was very close to Mrs. Roberts. She's looked after him all his life."

Beth glanced out the window of the shop. She could see Julian playing with some neighborhood children on the opposite sidewalk. The boy did not look upset. In fact, he was laughing.

Beth frowned, but only for a second. Had Julian caught her eye and continued laughing? Or had Beth imagined it? She looked back at Ian.

"Maybe you should spend a little more time with him," Beth suggested.

Ian nodded. "I'm planning to. That's exactly what I've decided. God, Beth, he's my son and he's been through a hell of a lot for an eight year old. Two horrible deaths in just a few weeks."

"I know," Beth comforted him.

"And he had to witness both of them," Ian continued. His voice sounded choked. "I mean it was bloody."

"What are you doing tomorrow?"

"Me?"

"You and Julian. Why don't we have a picnic? I know a great place. It's not far from here. Nobody will be there, just the three of us."

Ian waved a hand at the interior of the scrimshaw shop. "What about this place?"

"Don't worry about this place. I have part-time help on Saturday. Let them be full-time."

Ian seemed genuinely touched by Beth's generosity. He rose from his rocker and gave her a little hug.

"Thanks, Beth. I think Julian will really appreciate this."

When Ian exited the shop a short time later, Julian was still playing with the local boys. Beth watched from the window as the boy spied his father and immediately stopped his activity with the other youths. Julian ran to Ian.

Ian put his arm around the boy and led him off down the street. The children waved to Julian. He waved back dismissively.

One of the children called out to him.

"See you later, Bobo."

Startled, Ian jerked Julian around.

"What did he just call you?" Ian demanded.

Julian looked casual. "Who?"

"That kid there. He just called you Bobo.

Why did he call you that?"

Julian shrugged his shoulders innocently. "I like it. It's my nickname."

"Your nickname? Where did it come from?"

"I picked it." Julian sounded proud.

"Why that name?" Ian asked, his voice growing louder. "Why did you pick that name?"

Julian moved back from his father. "It's just a name, Daddy. I like the way it sounds. Bobo. Bobo."

Ian tightened his grip on the boy's shoulders. He was barely controlling his anger.

"Julian, I don't ever want to hear that name again. Do you understand me?"

The boy didn't answer.

Julian shook him violently. "Do you understand me?"

Again, Julian made no reply. Instead he merely looked in his father's eyes.

To Beth, watching all of this from the shop window, there was something evil there. An evil glint in the boy's fierce stare. She found herself drawing the window shade, just to shut that evil out.

Midnight on the water. A beach drenched in the full moon's bath. Waves choppy, violent, timeless. Evil lapping at the extremities of nature.

Close by, the Bellamy house stood outlined against the night sky. Stars blinked down, helpless witnesses to the doings of man. Already extinguished beacons, nothing more than silent reminders of the past.

There were no lights on in the house. In the master bedroom, the moon's light revealed Ian asleep under some light covers. He tossed fitfully, a prisoner of his own dreams.

One shaft of moonlight seemed to reach like an arm to the bedroom's open door. Then down the corridor—to where Julian, dressed in blue pajamas, emerged from his bedroom.

He moved toward the door that would take him below.

Evil lapping at nature's extremities. Work to be done downstairs.

The basement was cold, damp and uninviting. The beam of Julian's flashlight picked out a furnace, a boiler and a shiny new freezer.

Holding the flashlight chest high, Julian came carefully down the steps. He shone the light around. Exposed pipes everywhere.

The boy reached the bottom of the stairs. He stopped abruptly. He listened.

A loud squeal broke the dark silence. A rat dropped from the pipe above Julian, flashed past his face, hit the floor and scurried away. Julian didn't even react.

He walked over to the largest of the water pipes. Taking a wrench, he unscrewed the main valve and loosened the washer behind it. Water started to drip immediately.

Julian loosened the washer more, so that

water fell in a steady stream. He replaced the main valve.

Satisfied with his handiwork, Julian smiled. He crept quietly back upstairs.

Drip. Drip. Drip.

A puddle began to form on the basement floor.

"Ian, why are you standing in the water? Why don't you come upstairs?"

It was ten o'clock the next morning. Beth was at the top of the basement stairs, hollering down from the kitchen. The basement was three feet deep in water. Ian, wearing rubber hip boots, was standing in the flood, looking annoyed and helpless.

"Well, I've stopped the leak," Ian reported. "Now we just have to wait for the plumber. That could be a week from Tuesday."

Beth looked sympathetic. Behind her, at the kitchen table, Julian sat beside a large, over-stuffed picnic basket that Beth had provided. The boy appeared unperturbed.

"Maybe we should get some buckets and start bailing," Beth suggested.

Ian shook his head. "I think it'll drain, but the plumber said to wait."

"Fine," Beth agreed. "Why don't we have the picnic upstairs? Looks like rain anyway."

"Don't be silly, my darling. It's beautiful out."

Julian appeared in the doorway. His face had gone from a look of boredom to one of appar-ent disappointment.

"Does this mean we can't go on the picnic?" There was a childish whine in his voice.

Beth and Ian exchanged glances. Ian looked at the boy sympathetically.

"I have to hang around here, Julian," he said. "I'm sorry."

"You said we could go," Julian said petulantly. "You promised."

Beth glanced at Julian skeptically, then turned back toward Ian, who seemed taken in by the boy's show of disappointment.

"I've got an idea," Ian said. "I'll call the plumber again. Money talks around here. I'll offer him something extra. You guys go on the picnic. I'll meet you later."

Julian brightened immediately. "Oh, thank you, Daddy, thank you!"

"Sure you don't mind?" Beth asked hesitantly.

Ian splashed water. "No, go ahead. Save me a piece of fried chicken."

Julian disappeared into the kitchen.

Chapter Thirty-Eight

It was a steel-blue sunny day. The sky was lined with long, puffy clouds, which looked like heavenly cigar smoke that refused to move along.

Beth, behind the wheel, made up for the clouds' stationary mood.

Beth steered the car deftly along the wooded road. Ahead, in the distance, the trees grew denser. Julian sat beside her on the front seat, staring vacantly at the passing trees.

"I didn't know you like picnics so much, Julian." It was the fifth time Beth had tried to engage the boy in casual conversation.

Julian continued staring. "This one's different," he said quietly.

Beth pulled the car up at the edge of the woods. She and Julian got out. Beth opened the back door and took out Julian's little red wagon. Julian put the picnic basket and the blanket in it. Beth and Julian started into the woods. The boy tugged the wagon after him.

A half hour later, Beth and Julian were picking at the last remains of their lunch. They were sprawled out on the blanket, playing the card game War. The stack of cards and coins in front of Julian showed who was winning easily.

Beside Julian lay his trusty flute.

Beth turned over her last card, a queen. Julian nonchalantly topped it with an ace. He collected Beth's card and looked at her with a cruel half smile.

"You're not very lucky, are you, Beth?"

"That's only three games," Beth protested. "I'd like a rematch."

Julian shuffled the cards. But instead of splitting them up, he returned them to their box.

"My mother wasn't lucky either. Ian thinks you can replace her."

Beth eyed the boy with surprise. "And?"

Julian gave her a thin smile. "Catherine was much prettier."

"I'm sure your mother was lovely."

"*Is* lovely," Julian corrected her.

"Yes, of course. But we don't replace one another. That's not what life is all about."

"No?" Julian asked innocently.

"What do you say we play some checkers?" Beth suggested. "I'm very good at checkers."

Julian stared her down. "Did you ever wish for something?"

"Yes. Everybody wishes."

"Catherine used to wish all the time. That's the reason I'm here. Catherine wished me."

Beth looked a bit frightened. She tried to set up the checkerboard.

"What will it be? Red or black?"

"Did you hear what I said? *Catherine wished me.*"

"You mean she wanted you? She wanted a child?"

Julian shook his head slowly. "She didn't want a child. Not at first. Ian wanted a child. Catherine was happy having *me*."

"I don't understand." Beth was having difficulty sorting the red checkers from the black ones. "Aren't you a child?"

"Catherine's child died in the womb," Julian said patiently. It was as though he were an adult talking to a child. "Catherine cried out for me. I'm the replacement."

Beth was confused. "For the baby?"

"For Catherine," Julian hissed angrily at her. "She wished me. I'm here to make Ian pay. He hurt her. He made her die."

Julian picked up the flute. He stared at it. He looked back toward Beth.

"You mean a great deal to Ian," the boy continued. "He worships you."

"I've heard enough of this."

Julian leaned closer across the blanket.

250

"Why don't you show me what you show Ian, you whore?"

The boy began playing his familiar melody on the flute. Beth was frozen in terror. And then seemingly under Julian's control, Beth began to unbutton her blouse.

Julian continued playing. The musical notes danced under his fingers like the flashes of sunlight on the ground.

Beth removed her blouse. Julian looked at her bare breasts with contempt.

"Get up," he ordered.

Dazed, Beth rose to her feet, dropping the red and black checkers. She wore only her skirt.

"Dance for me, you whore."

The boy resumed his flute playing. Beth began a slow dance in the clearing. Julian noted her steps with casual interest.

His fingers moved quickly over the flute. Beth began to dance more rapidly.

Her bare feet crashed up and down on the hard earth. She was approaching a frenzy as Julian's musical accompaniment stepped up the tempo.

Blood poured from Beth's feet. One of her toes snapped like a twig in the forest.

Beth spun wildly toward the trees that ringed the clearing. Still fingering the flute holes, Julian struck the pose of a choreographer, one leg straight, the other bent slightly.

As though choreographing Beth's mad dance,

Julian propelled her toward a giant maple tree.

It was an old tree, but not as old as Evil.

Julian summoned up vast resources of energy from a power as old as time itself. He directed that power to a dazed, frightened, whirling Beth Wellman, who hit the maple tree, bounced off, then returned to bash her face repeatedly against the rough bark of the thick trunk.

Julian laughed through his flute playing as Beth caromed off the maple and spun away toward a red-leafed elm.

So great was her centrifugal force that Beth's feet no longer touched the ground.

She smashed her pretty face against the elm. Blood flew from her broken nose. Beth looked terrified, but unable to stop the damage she was doing to her face by smashing it into the tree trunk.

Julian was still playing the flute.

Beth had shattered most of her teeth. One of her eyes was hanging from its socket. Julian grinned and stepped up the tempo.

Screaming wildly, Beth continued to inflict harm to her head, which was bleeding in gushers. Blood covered her shoulders and breasts. Her skirt, which had ripped apart with her earliest gyrations, lay on the ground like a tattered flag of defeat.

With one vicious bash, Beth smashed her once-lovely face completely out of recognition. Now it was pulp.

Animus

She fell to the ground in her death agony. Julian finished his tune as Beth finished her life.

Later, the boy loaded Beth's lifeless body into his little red wagon. He collected the remainder of the picnic items and put them in the basket. Covering Beth's corpse with the blanket, he placed the basket on top. Tugging the wagon behind him, he set off for home.

Chapter Thirty-Nine

"Well, this is a surprise. You're a little late to bail water, but you can watch me pay the plumber."

Still in his hip boots, a surprised Ian greeted Dr. Janet Parker, who had turned up at his kitchen door.

Ian handed a check to the plumber, a taciturn Nantucketer who pocketed the slip of paper after a quick scan of its numerical figure.

As the plumber left, Ian motioned for Dr. Parker to accompany him back downstairs. Once in the newly dry basement, Ian began washing his hands at the sink. Janet sat down on one of the bottom steps.

"How's Julian?" she asked.

"Julian? Oh, he's fine. He's off on a picnic."

"I heard about Mrs. Roberts. I'm sorry."

Ian didn't answer. He poured more cleansing powder on his hands and scrubbed them vigorously under the faucet.

"I'm a little worried about Julian. That's why I came up here."

"I thought you didn't make house calls."

Janet considered the remark for a moment. Next to the stairs was a ledge that contained several cardboard cartons. Catherine's name was written on the side of one of the boxes. At the top of the carton was a red scrapbook. Absently, Janet lifted it out of the box. On the front, in large block letters, were the words *Bobo's Book*.

Her fingers suddenly trembling, Janet opened the book. She stifled a cry.

Inside was a portrait of Bobo, signed by Catherine and dated 25 years earlier. It was a perfect likeness of Julian.

Dr. Parker slid the red scrapbook under her purse. Just then, she realized that Ian had turned from the sink and was looking at her expectantly.

"This isn't exactly a house call," she heard herself saying. "I think there is something very strange going on that involves Julian."

"Oh?" Ian was moving closer.

"When I drove up here, I was just following my instinct. But I just found something you might want to have a look at."

255

Janet reached beneath her purse and withdrew the book. She handed it to Ian. He looked at the cover.

"Where did you find this?"

Janet pointed to the nearby ledge. "Right there. It was on top of that carton."

"I'll bet Julian has seen this cover," Ian said thoughtfully. "That would explain it."

"Explain what?"

"Why he's chosen Bobo as a nickname."

Janet was startled. "I don't think so."

Ian opened the book. As his dark eyes skidded over the drawing, it was his turn to look startled.

Janet decided to press the advantage. "That drawing of Bobo was done when Catherine was eight years old. Even as an adult, she used to remember it in her dreams. In one of our sessions, she told me how she sat in a meadow and painted Bobo's picture. You see who it resembles?"

"Yes," Ian responded soberly.

"Catherine also told me that, after she finished the drawing, she and Bobo went to play on the swings. I haven't looked, but turn the page."

Ian obeyed. On the following page, there was a snapshot of Catherine as a child. She was sitting on a swing, smiling contentedly. Behind her was a blurred image that seemed to be pushing the swing. The image resembled Julian.

"Jesus Christ," Ian muttered.

With a loud bang, Julian appeared at the top of the stairs, looking innocent.

Trying to hide his alarm, Ian said, "How long have you been home?"

"A couple minutes." He looked strangely at the ceiling. "I had something to do upstairs."

"Isn't Beth with you?"

"Beth's no fun. She got a headache."

With a quick dart of the eyes toward Janet, Ian closed the scrapbook and slid it from view.

Chapter Forty

A few minutes later, Julian sat across the kitchen table from Janet. He had a glass of chocolate milk in front of him. Janet had made herself a cup of coffee. The kitchen door was shut, giving the two of them some privacy.

"Do you remember the last time we talked?" Dr. Parker began.

"Yes."

"You mentioned a nightmare that your mother used to have. About your grandfather. Who told you about that?"

Julian met her eyes. "Nobody."

"Then how are you aware of it?"

Julian gave a ghostly smile. "I think you know."

The door opened. Ian walked into the kitchen.

"Sorry to interrupt. Julian, you did say that Beth went home, didn't you?"

"Yes."

"That's funny. I just tried her number and there's no answer. Maybe I'll take a run over there, see how she feels. She's probably just not answering."

"Fine," Janet said. "We'll be here."

"See you in a little while."

Ian closed the door behind him. Janet waited until she heard his car start up in the driveway before she continued.

"I know a few things, Julian. I know about your nickname. Bobo. Your mother had a friend named Bobo. An imaginary playmate."

Julian's look was cold and knowing. "Imaginary? You mean her Animus."

Janet was taken aback. "That's a big word for a little boy."

Julian played with the spoon next to his chocolate milk. "I'm *not* a little boy."

Janet took the scrapbook from beside her chair. She opened it to the drawing.

"You look like this little boy."

Julian glanced at the picture and smiled.

"Your mother drew this when she was eight years old."

Julian nodded. "I remember."

"You remember?"

Julian was looking away, as though through a window into the past.

"We were in a field. We went to play on the swing."

Janet showed him the photograph. "This swing?"

The boy's smile broadened. "Catherine liked the swing. I used to push her and she'd fly up really high. She wasn't afraid. She felt that no one could hurt her up there."

"You protected her?"

"Yes. Except at the end. Ian hurt her and there was nothing I could do."

"You call yourself Bobo."

"I am Bobo," the boy corrected her.

"Do you believe that you are Catherine's Animus?"

Julian's eyes blazed into her. "Don't you?"

Janet wanted to look away, but couldn't. "I don't know. Animus is just a theory. Imaginary playmates don't come to life."

"Catherine wished it. She thought she was dying. She needed me. She willed me into life."

"Why?" Janet asked. She felt dizzy, disoriented by the boy's gaze, his otherworldly manner.

Julian stood up suddenly. He moved about the room purposefully. Little stabs of fear went into Janet's heart.

"To hurt the people that hurt her," Julian explained. "Make them pay for what they did to her. Ian hurt Catherine inside. He'll be sorry. She would have had a normal baby." Julian bowed his head. "But it died."

"You mean the twin?"

"There was no twin." There was a layer of menace in the eight year old's voice. "Catherine cried out for me. I'm part of her. She died and I was born."

Dr. Parker tried to think rationally. "If you're Catherine's Animus, you're not even a person. You're not real."

"What I did to Catherine's father was real."

Janet felt panic. Blood icy as steel coursed through her veins. "Oh, my God."

"What I did to Mrs. Roberts was real."

Janet stared in shock. "Mrs. Roberts never did anything to Catherine."

Julian raised an eyebrow. "She got in the way."

Janet looked around. It was time to get out of there, out of that room, that house, that island.

As though reading her mind, Julian slammed his small fist on the kitchen table.

"Sit down. I want you to see something."

The boy lifted the receiver on the kitchen wall phone. He dialed the operator.

Suddenly, he shot into hysteria, a matchless impression of a boy in terror.

"Operator? This is Julian Bishop at the Bellamy house." His voice cracked. Tears spurted from his eyes. "Call the police! Something horrible has happened. Oh, please, please, it's horrible!"

Calmly, he hung up the phone. The tears

ceased as quickly as they had begun. Julian had shut them off as one would a torrent from a faucet. Pleased with his performance, he looked over at Janet Parker.

"Why did you do that?" she asked.

Julian's face was a map of hell's landscape. "You'll see."

Ian's car roared down the island road, took a corner at high speed and shot across the other lane to pull up outside Beth's scrimshaw shop.

Ian jumped from the vehicle and hurried toward the store. He spotted a sign in the window: *Closed For Lunch*. Ian fumbled in his pants pockets for the keys. He found them and let himself into the shop.

"Beth?"

Ian called her name cautiously as his eyes took in the front room. No sign of Beth. Ian padded toward the back of the store. He stopped. His eyes darted about.

Beth wasn't there either.

Chapter Forty-One

"Why are you telling me all this?" Janet Parker asked.

She and Julian were in the Bellamy house kitchen. Julian leaned against the counter in a grown-up's stance, looking at Janet with a superior expression. Janet was trying to keep calm, but not doing a very good job of it.

"Catherine was no liar." Julian's voice was quiet but forceful. "I want you to know I exist."

Janet nodded her head. "You are manifest."

"I am Bobo. It took me eight years to get strong enough to do what I have to do."

Janet remembered something from a long-ago session in her West End Avenue office.

"Catherine was eight when you first appeared." Janet paused. "What if I tried to stop you?"

Julian eyed her coldly. "You can't stop me. Besides, who would ever believe you?"

A smile crossed Julian's face. For an instant, he looked away. Janet made a run for it.

Heart thumping, one shoe already sent flying, Dr. Parker raced from the kitchen. In seconds, she was tearing down the front steps toward her black Mercedes. Thank God it was still in the drive. Janet tore open the car door. She slid in behind the steering wheel.

But Julian was nearly to the car. His eyes blazed with ferocious evil.

The keys.

Where were the fucking keys? In the ignition. Oh, please, God, in the ignition. Janet Parker's eyes flew to the ignition keyhole.

No keys. They were back in her purse. In the kitchen. Now what?

All at once, Julian's face popped up at the car's side window. He jabbed a meat cleaver through the open window. It narrowly missed Janet's face.

Terrified, Dr. Parker threw herself across the front seat. She squeezed open the far side door and jumped out of the car. Only inches from a diving Julian.

Janet kicked away her other shoe and ran down the drive. Rocks and clumps of dirt pounded the balls of her feet with each step.

She was almost to the road. Thank God she had longer legs than Julian.

But Julian was gaining. He waved the meat cleaver in the air. It flashed with sunburst.

From far off in the distance, Janet could hear a car approaching. Maybe the driver would stop and help her. But Julian was almost there. Janet ducked down.

If I can just hide from him. . . .

Janet scurried from the road into a nearby wooded thicket. She ducked down behind some shrubs that were overrun with tall grass.

She tried to catch her breath.

The forest was bathed in soft warm sunshine. Birds dove and rose among the branches. Julian was still stalking his prey, the meat cleaver cradled at his chest like a beloved artifact.

Janet cowered behind the shrubs.

He doesn't see me. Oh, if only he doesn't see me.

A few yards away, Julian had indeed lost her. His eyes moved methodically in his head, scanning the forest area. His expression was one of infinite patience.

He turned around. Then, as if following some primitive instinct older than earth itself, he walked right toward where Janet Parker knelt huddled in the tall grass.

When he was only ten yards away, Janet made a dash for her life.

Panic. Sheer panic. Janet's legs churned beneath her as she tried to will herself out of

Julian's demonic clutches. But as she rushed through the underbrush, branches tearing at her skin, the boy was gaining on her.

She could hear the steady stride of his feet coming closer. She dared not look back but . . . *he was only inches away!*

Janet threw her entire body forward. She never saw the log.

Thump.

The toes of Janet's right foot hit the log squarely, sending pain up and down her body. Janet was catapulted forward. It was impossible not to fall. She arched her back as if she were going over a high jump. That movement righted her. Janet didn't fall.

Thump.

Julian fell instead. His attention diverted by Janet's stumble forward, the boy had never seen the log. He lay in a bed of dry leaves, looking stunned.

Janet Parker kept going. She was nearly to the road. The approaching car she had heard moments earlier was close by. She could hear its engine in the near distance. It was going slower, as if it were turning off toward the woods.

Not far behind Janet, Julian scrambled to his feet. He resumed his pursuit, his face a brutal fist of anger.

Janet reached the road just as Ian's car was passing. She tried to summon up strength to call out.

Animus

He didn't see me.

The vehicle disappeared down the tree-hooded road. Janet looked around, brushing tears from her face.

Julian was on top of her.

Chapter Forty-Two

Something's happened to Beth.

Those four words echoed violently in Ian Bishop's brain as he drove feverishly down the woodland dirt road toward the Bellamy house.

A moment ago, out of the corner of his eye, Ian had thought he'd seen something moving among the trees. A flash of color. He might have heard a sound. Someone crying out, maybe. No use stopping. It was probably nothing. He had to get to the house.

Something's happened to Beth.

Ian's mind was on a narrow track. Beth's face swam before him—eyes dancing, lips smiling. Head thrown back in a burst of laughter. Some innocent joke, long forgotten, from a happier time.

Animus

Don't rush, darling. You're much too late.

Ian floored the gas pedal. Trees were flying by the car, their branches whipping against the window like lashes.

Had someone just spoken to him?

Ian's ears seemed to be filling up with water. The roar of waves cascaded in his head.

Don't rush. She's much too dead.

What was that? Who was that?

Ian tried to pray. He fought to remember prayers from his childhood. He could retrieve nothing that would replace the words that kept clattering in his skull like nails in a glass box.

Something's happened to Beth.

No. Not Beth. She was all that was wonderful in his life. Everything else—money, prestige, power—was just a sham.

Ian could see the Bellamy house emerge from the trees up ahead.

If only he could remember some prayers. There was one. . . .

Now and at the hour of our death. Amen.

Something laughed childishly in Ian Bishop's frantic brain.

Ian slammed on the brakes in front of the house. He leaped from the car and bounded up the front steps.

The living room was strangely quiet. An eerie feeling of dread was beginning to seep into Ian's pores. Seeing the door to the kitchen open, Ian went over and peered inside.

Janet's purse and the scrapbook were on the kitchen table.

Not that way. The other way.

A voice was in Ian's head. A voice that sounded strangely familiar.

Without thinking, Ian spun around. He went through the silent living room to the corridor that led toward the master bedroom. In a moment, Ian was at the door to the room he had once shared with Catherine.

His hand went to the doorknob.

Open it, darling.

Ian turned the knob.

The bedroom was still. Strangely dark. Light filtered through the gauzy curtains, diffusing the image of the bloody, mutilated corpse that was splayed out like a discarded rag doll on the large double bed.

Ian moved toward the bed, his eyes fluttering in the opaque light.

Don't you see her?

Ian spied the reflection of Beth in the dresser mirror. He began to gag. He turned. He went to her. As he touched her bare shoulder, she pitched forward on the bed.

Ian was backing out of the room. His hand was over his mouth. His expression was one of abject horror. In a state of shock, he backed down the corridor toward the living room.

A loud noise made Ian spin around.

Janet had run into the house. She stood there at the entrance to the living room. The noise was the slamming door she hoped would keep Julian out.

Janet's eyes went to Ian. She looked instantly relieved. Then fearful.

"Oh, God. Oh, God," Ian choked on the words. "It's Beth. It's Beth."

Janet heard a clamor from the side of the house. That must be Julian, she thought in a panic, coming in the kitchen door.

Dazed, Ian sank down onto the sofa. His eyes were staring wildly at nothing.

"She's dead," he said, his voice barely above a whisper. "Her face, it's all. . . ."

Janet wrenched her eyes from Ian. Julian was standing in the doorway. He smiled at her triumphantly.

Enraged, Janet dove across the room. She grabbed Julian by the collar. She shook him violently.

"Beth never hurt Catherine," Janet heard herself screaming. "Why?"

Julian shook himself loose. He pointed at Ian. He spoke in a soft murmur so his father wouldn't hear.

"*He* wanted her."

Horrified, Janet stepped back. On the couch, Ian looked up. He noticed Julian for the first time. He got to his feet slowly and approached the boy.

"Julian," Ian said gravely. "Thank God you're all right."

Ian went to embrace him. Janet came between the two of them.

"Don't touch him!" she shrieked. "He killed her! He killed Mr. Bellamy! He killed Mrs. Roberts! He's a monster. He's not even real. He's Bobo! Don't touch him. He's Bobo!"

Ian looked at Janet Parker with pity. The poor woman had finally snapped, he thought. He embraced Julian. At least he still had his son.

Unseen by Ian, Julian smirked at Janet, who looked defeated.

The doorbell rang.

Janet ran to open the door. She admitted two uniformed policemen into the living room.

When she turned, she saw that Julian had quickly extricated himself from Ian's embrace. The boy was already crying hysterically. He ran to the cops and hid behind them.

One of the officers, a burly, mustached red-head, stepped forward.

"We got a phone call," he announced. "Some kind of a disturbance."

Before anyone could speak, Julian pointed an accusing finger at Ian.

"He did it. He did it. He killed her! Oh, Daddy, Daddy, why did you do it? You killed Beth! She's in the bedroom. You killed her!"

"Where's the bedroom?" the cop asked matter-of-factly.

Still feigning hysteria, Julian pointed down the hall. The second cop moved off in that direction.

Animus

Ian looked bewildered. "Julian, what are you saying?"

Janet, realizing what Julian was trying to do, grabbed the remaining cop by the shoulders. She pointed at Julian.

"He's lying! He killed her! He's killed three people! He tried to kill me!"

The cop frowned. "Hold on a minute."

"You've got to believe me," Janet continued. "I'm a doctor. The boy is evil. He's not real. He killed Beth. He told me!"

The other cop reappeared from the bedroom. His face was ashen. "Lady," he said, "I just took a look at that corpse. No little boy could do that."

Chapter Forty-Three

The next few days were a fast-forward night-mare. Ian could not even recall the trip back down to New York. Somehow, he was in his own apartment. Somehow, Ian, Michael and Janet sat somberly in the Bishop living room. They toyed with their cocktails. The sun was going down.

Ian looked haggard. He had not slept very much in the past five days. Still, he was impeccably turned out. Dressed for success. Groomed to within an inch of his life.

On the coffee table in front of them was a tabloid newspaper with a bold front-page head-line in red: *Art Dealer Free on Bail in Sweetheart's Slaying*. Below, in a subhead: *Son in Protective Custody*.

Running vertically down the side of the front page was a photograph of a smiling Beth in a bikini. The picture had been taken when she was in college, long before she'd met Ian Bishop. But that newspaper was not known for accuracy or even coherence.

Ian scowled at the headline. "Protective custody. What's that supposed to mean?"

Michael tried not to sound like a lawyer. "It means they don't want you to talk to him. They don't want you to see him."

"They think I'd want to hurt him, right?" Ian's eyes were wide, almost boyish.

"Who knows what they think? They've got to be careful."

"He's my son. I would never hurt him. I just want to find out why he's lying."

Janet stirred in her chair. "He's not your son. He's Catherine's Animus. He's Bobo."

Ian stared out the window. Birds were perched on the window ledge outside, the ledge where Julian had played with a girl his age on his birthday.

"I don't accept that, Janet. I'm sorry. I cannot believe that my son isn't real."

Janet shook her head solemnly. "He isn't real. Not the way we define reality."

Michael's eyes issued a warning. "I'm afraid his testimony is going to be very real."

"Well, I'm prepared to counteract that testimony," Dr. Parker said forcefully. "Julian told me he killed Mr. Bellamy. And Mrs. Roberts. And Beth."

Ian's laugh was hollow. "Wonderful, Janet. Three people murdered by an imaginary playmate. Who's going to believe that?"

An hour later, Ian was alone in the living room. Looking forlorn, he peered through the window curtains, down to the street where Janet and Michael were just emerging from the building. The doorman flagged down a taxi. Ian's two friends got into the same cab, which drove away.

That's nice, Ian thought, they can share a taxi. They have lives to go back to.

Ian turned back from the window. He went to the bar and freshened his drink. Three whiskey sours in the last 90 minutes, but he felt nothing.

What was that?

Something light. Melodic. Possibly music. Coming from nearby. In the apartment.

A flute.

Ian put down his drink. He listened.

This couldn't be.

The familiar melody that Catherine had composed as a child was wafting through the Bishop apartment. Softly at first, but insistent.

Ian began to tremble. Shakily, tentatively, with fear in his very bones, he walked toward the hallway.

Ian went slowly along the corridor. The sound of the flute was growing louder. Ian was nearly at the bedroom door. It was closed.

The way it should be at that time. Cocktail hour. Doors closed to the private rooms.

Open it.

Ian obeyed. Slowly, he turned the glass doorknob. Gently, he pushed the door inward.

Julian's bedroom was dark except for a shard of bloody sun that came through the window.

Blinding. Can't see anything.

The flute music ceased.

Ian reached for the light switch. His fingers were moist with sweat and fear.

Click.

Julian was sitting on the bed, holding the flute, naked, next to the portrait of Bobo that Catherine had painted as a child.

"Hello, Daddy."

Ian blinked at the incoming light. He was frozen in the doorway, shocked and bewildered, his hand still resting on the glass knob.

"How? I don't understand. . . ."

Julian sliced the air with his hand. "No, you don't understand. You never have. Catherine told you about me many times. But you didn't believe her. You said I was a figment of her imagination. Do you still believe that, Ian?"

Ian's voice was ragged, barely audible. "I believe you're my son. I want to know why you're making up lies about me, why you want to see me in prison."

"I don't want to see you in prison," Julian corrected him calmly. "I didn't kill three people so you could go to prison. I've got something better planned for you."

Ian took a small step forward. "You didn't kill anyone. You need help, Julian. I just want to help you."

Julian ran his fingers the length of the flute. "Like you helped Catherine?"

"I loved Catherine."

Julian's reply was drenched in cold fury. "Loved her? You never even knew her. I knew her as nobody else knew her. I knew her from inside. I'm Catherine's Animus."

Ian tried to take another step. No use. He was immobile with fear.

"I want to show you something," Julian said. "Remember how beautiful Catherine was? Her skin? So soft. Her breasts? Warm. Inviting."

Something began to happen before Ian's astonished eyes.

Julian put down the flute. He stretched his body languorously on the freshly made bed. How big my boy is getting, Ian thought through all his confusion.

How big my boy is getting.

Julian's frame seemed to extend from the pillows all the way down to the foot of the bed. His legs, gangly like a boy's but with touches of baby fat a moment earlier, seemed oddly rounded, more complete, longer, lithe, sensuous. . . .

As though hypnotized, Ian's eyes went to Julian's torso. Something was happening there.

What had been an eight year old's skinny chest had blossomed into something fuller, more robust, inviting. . . .

Ian looked up. Julian's face was moving subtly. Ian felt as if he was watching a photographic process, a time-lapse change that was rendering his son into something else, something with long chestnut hair and hazel eyes. . . .

And luscious waiting lips. . . .

And ripe breasts. . . .

And. . . .

"You thought her body was perfect," Julian hissed. "You couldn't wait to make love to her. Wouldn't you like to make love to her one more time?"

The transformation was complete. The figure of Catherine, sexy and enticing, rose slowly to its feet. She smiled lovingly at Ian.

"Take me, darling."

"Catherine," Ian whispered.

Woodenly, he went toward her. It. Whatever was there.

The creature held out her arms as though to embrace him. Ian drew nearer, not fully believing, but wanting to. Suddenly, he was touching her. It felt like . . . *Catherine*.

The thing was in his arms. Ian was reaching for it with his lips. Its mouth was seeking his. They kissed, tenderly, their mouths converging as they had so many times before when Catherine was . . . *alive*.

As their tongues intertwined, Catherine's eyeball began to drop from its socket until finally it hung by only a tendon. His eyes pressed closed in rediscovered ecstasy, Ian failed to notice the transformation that was happening.

Catherine's other eye popped loose from its moorings and shot out on its wiry tendon.

Ian stirred in his passion. A flicker that something was wrong sent his eyelids fluttering.

A repulsive black bile resembling sludge from an automobile engine began trickling from the side of Catherine's mouth. Ian's eyes were fully open. He jumped back, startled. A cry started from his mouth, but fizzled into silence.

Bile poured from Catherine's mouth as though being pumped hydraulically from inside. In a matter of seconds, Ian was covered with the pitch-black sludge.

All over Catherine's nude body, her skin began to erupt. Bubbles formed beneath the surface of her skin, grew larger, then burst in lavalike liquid.

Ian's eyes were saucers of horror and fear. His feet were frozen to the spot.

As he watched in terror, Catherine's belly shook with a jagged spasm. Suddenly, it began to enlarge. Her stomach was expanding like some grotesque balloon being inflated. Like a fast-action photograph, Catherine was changing from a lithe and statuesque beauty to the equivalent of a bloated, unappealing pregnant woman. Close to bursting.

Animus

As quickly as it had begun, the expansion stopped.

Catherine stood perfectly still. She set her legs apart.

Suddenly, her belly began to deflate. Slowly at first, then faster. From between her legs emerged something that made Ian's entire body shake with horror.

Out of Catherine's womb came a bile-drenched form in the shape of a newborn child. A throbbing baby from hell that hung angrily from a whiplike umbilical cord as Ian gagged in terror.

Ian backed wordlessly toward the bedroom door. No sound could come from him. Nearby, the portrait of Bobo smoldered and began to disintegrate.

Farther west, in Janet Parker's office, as moonlight streamed through the windows onto her desk, the photograph of Catherine and Bobo on the swings began to burn and fall apart.

Chapter Forty-Four

Two weeks later, Dr. Janet Parker was driving north on the New York State Thruway, headed toward central Connecticut. A dull, steady rain was falling. Michael Spinoza was beside Janet in the front seat. The windshield wipers moved like metronomes across the water-splattered glass.

After driving for some time in silence, Janet spoke, trying to sound casual.

"Well, we're going to meet Nicky today. What do you think that will be like?"

Michael glanced at her. "You tell me."

Janet paused. The rain swept off the windshield, only to be replaced instantly. "I don't know. He hasn't been around in a long time."

They rode on for several moments. Neither spoke.

"I was just thinking about Julian," Michael said. "Where do you think he is?"

"Gone." Janet sounded positive.

"Gone? You mean dead?"

"No. I mean gone."

"Follow me."

Mr. Vickers, the darkly clad director of the institution, led Janet and Michael down the long corridor of the facility. Their footsteps echoed sharply in the deserted hallway, which was buffed to a mirror sheen.

Vickers stopped before a heavy white door, at the top of which was a small barred window.

"I'm afraid this is as far as you can go," Mr. Vickers reminded them.

"Yes." Michael nodded. "We know."

Janet and Michael pressed their faces to the narrow, barred window. Through it, they could see a contained, white-padded cell.

"Oh, my God," Janet Parker breathed.

Ian Bishop was standing in the farthest corner of the cell. He was dressed in loose-fitting sanitorium whites. He had aged ten years since Janet and Michael had last seen him.

Ian spoke in a haunted voice that was just audible to them through the heavy, locked door. Ian's voice retained the rhythms of childhood. He was oblivious to the two visitors whose faces filled his only window.

"They can't see you, Nicky," Ian said. "I don't know why they can't see you. They don't believe you're real. They're just silly. We don't need them anyway."

Outside, Janet Parker had begun to cry. Michael put an arm around her comfortingly. In the white-padded cell, Ian's voice rose slightly, assuming an eerie singsong quality:

"Nicky's my buddy.
Nicky's my friend.
I'll stay with Nicky,
Right to the end."

Ian began turning slowly in the corner of his room, doing a childlike dance to music only he could hear. His brow was furrowed with concentration. He was hopelessly mad.

At midnight, Julian sat beneath a willow tree in a garden near Gramercy Park. His fingers were on a flute. His eyes were on a square of window in the nearby Hart Clinic.

A night-light burned in that window, casting a soft glow on the glass that only Julian could see. His mother was behind that glass, lying immobile, hooked up to hospital machinery that monitored her every feeble breath.

Breath that stirred as Julian's flute song rose from the garden. Breath that gained strength as the musical notes were lofted up above the willow tree.

There was no time. There were no senses. There was darkness. . . .

And then there was light.

SPECIAL SNEAK PREVIEW!

COMING IN NOVEMBER 1993!

THE OTHERS
By David Wind

Our story so far...

An aberration in space and time, the doorways link worlds and dimensions that were never supposed to meet. And for hundreds of years, shapeshifters have been trapped on earth, desperately seeking the portal that will return them to their own world. Although their fate has brought them the gift of immortality, the otherworlders are cursed with ever-increasing insanity the longer they stay on this planet. Hoping to discover the secret of the aliens' abilities for their own ends, U.S. government agents have imprisoned a group of the otherworlders—but their power play may result in the annihilation of all mankind....

Don't miss *The Others*!
On sale at newsstands and bookstores everywhere in November 1993.

Sperry Hollow,
Virginia.

The office was soundproof, which suited Amos Aldredge's purposes. The walls were off-white. No pictures broke the sterile plainness. The room's single window was covered by closed, white vertical blinds. The overhead light was fluorescent. Two chairs were set before the desk. Only one was occupied.

Aldredge sat behind the large desk. His salt-and-pepper hair made a striking counterpoint to his parchment-colored face, the color of a man who spends all his hours indoors. Moist and pale eyes, watery blue, gazed over the rims of silver, wire-framed glasses set low on a narrow nose. His lips were thinned into an angry slash.

"It was you, wasn't it?" he asked the man sitting across from him. The man's face was expressionless, his age indeterminable. He could have been 20 or 40. Only his green eyes showed any animation.

"Me?" Charles Langst replied. His gaze never wavered, his stoic expression remaining the same.

"Don't play games with me. We have an agreement. I've stuck by mine. You broke yours. It has to stop!"

"Amos," Langst began, his voice soothing, "I gave you my word, and I intended to abide by it. However, being shot wasn't part of our agreement."

"What the hell were you doing out of the compound?"

Charles Langst stared openly at him. "Having fun. I've been cooped up here for a long time. I needed a change, and I took it. As you know, I have many needs. At times, those needs must be fulfilled."

"You might have endangered the project."

"But I did not. And I will not have you calling me down for this. You know how to cover those things up. And," he added, cocking his head to the side, "I'm sure it's already been taken care of. After all, your government is very powerful."

"It can't happen again," Aldredge warned.

"They won't keep on cleaning up after you."

"Then keep your promise and get us home," Langst said. He stood, towering above the seated scientist. Looking malevolently down at the smaller man, he added, "Do it soon, or I won't be able to hold the others."

Amos Aldredge refused to be faced down. He stood and shook his head. "Don't threaten me, Charles. Don't ever threaten me."

Langst smiled. Within his soul, Amos Aldredge shivered, for he could almost see the canines growing.

"I don't threaten, Amos. I just do what is necessary. By the way," Langst said offhandedly, "keep your eye on Kali. She's made contact with someone."

"Contact? Impossible."

"Oh, she has. And nothing is impossible. You should know that by now."

"With whom? Another of your people?"

"No, he's not one of us."

"She hasn't been out of her room since her escape attempt. She couldn't contact anyone. How could she?"

Langst tapped an index finger against his temple. "We don't need phones. And, Amos, the one she's been in contact with is the man who was on the road the night Kali tried to . . . ah, escape."

Langst turned then, leaving Aldredge to stare after him. Once outside, Langst walked toward the building that housed him and his people.

He breathed deeply of the night air, drawing in a profusion of scents, many of which were undetectable to a normal person.

Pausing halfway to his destination, Langst looked up at the sky. He knew the sky and its stars well. In fact, there was no one alive on the face of this earth who knew it better than he. He was, he believed, the oldest survivor of his people.

He heard a truck in the distance. Turning, he gazed toward the sound. Headlights cut through the night, reflecting off the chain-link fence. Seeing the metal barriers so illuminated made Langst feel confined.

He needed to be free. He needed to range. He thought about Aldredge's pathetic warning and almost laughed. He needed the man, and the man needed him. But no one ever told him what he could or could not do. No one!

He started forward again, but instead of going to the building, he skirted it. When he was out of sight, he disrobed; then he inhaled deeply and shifted.

Seconds later, using the shape of a hawk, Langst rose high above the compound. He moved fast, riding the air currents to gain height. Below him the earth spread out in dark night contours. He leaned into the wind and let the currents take him with them.

To his left, Sperry Hollow glittered in the night. He fought his impulse to go there to hunt. Instead, he ranged on, looking for game that was not part of the area.

A half hour later he spotted a man walking along the darkened interstate. He was young, bearded and husky, and he was alone.

Langst looped above him and gave vent to the cry of a hawk, hunting.

When the man looked up, Langst dove. He swooped over the man, missing him by less than three feet. He felt pleasure at seeing the man duck even before he halted his swift dive.

Then he flew to a branch not 20 feet away. The man stared at him for a full minute before headlights broke the night.

The man turned to the road and held out his right hand, his thumb sticking almost straight up. Langst dropped to the ground. He stared at the man and slowly shifted again, almost casually as the scent of the man filled his nostrils.

The car didn't slow down for the hitchhiker. When the man turned back to the tree, his face registered relief at the vanished hawk.

Then Langst rose on all four legs and started toward the man. He'd chosen the form of a mastiff. He moved slowly, watching for the instant that the man would spot him. He halved the distance before the man's face tensed with recognition of the dog. The wind blew toward Langst. Not three seconds after the man spotted him, Langst smelled the fear seeping from the man's mind. He inhaled deeply and picked up his pace.

The hitchhiker turned and started to run.

Langst followed at a lope.

The man ran faster, looking over his shoulder frequently to check on Langst's progress.

Langst could feel the panic beginning to set into the man's mind. He was in no hurry and reveled in the smell of fear.

Langst increased his pace and the man ran faster. He could hear the man's tortured and gasping breaths. The sound and the fear fed Langst's mind and made his body tingle with expectation.

Langst did not rush but rather paced himself carefully. A quarter of a mile later, he was within a dozen feet of the man. He was teasing him, waiting for the man to reach that rare point when the pulsing fear that powered his feet would paralyze him and hold him in readiness for Langst to take him.

The growing fear fed Langst. It was fear that nourished him. It was fear that gave him his power over others. Fear was his drug—his heroin, his crack.

And it was in that last moment of consciousness, as his victims breathed their last gulps of air, that Charles Langst achieved a release so far above the sexual that he could only think of it as spiritual.

It was for that precise moment that he lived. The sensation of ultimate power—the knowledge that he had total control over the life and death of any living thing—was so intense and so important that he needed to have it more and more often. And he knew that nothing could stop him, ever, for he was truly the most superior being that this world had ever known.

The hitchhiker stumbled, fell and started up.

Langst stopped two feet from him. His dark green eyes locked onto the man's frightened blue eyes. Langst growled, saliva dripping from the corners of his mouth.

Langst's muscles bunched tightly. His rear legs coiled like a steel spring awaiting release. The man's fear was palpable. Langst breathed it in, sucking it deep down into his very being as he prepared to spring.

Before he could launch himself, a new set of headlights broke the darkness and pinned the fallen man. The man scrambled to his feet, waving frantically at the oncoming car.

The car slowed down, and Langst growled deep in his throat. When the car came to a stop, Langst howled once before running off into the trees that lined the side of the road.

An instant later his form coalesced into the human shape that was his from birth. He stood next to a tree and watched the man who he had been hunting get into the car. As the vehicle drove off, Langst saw the man stare back to where he stood.

Langst laughed, loud and harsh, until the sound grated in his ears. His temper was roiling. He needed release, and it had been taken from him. He had been thwarted, and he was angry. He still needed to hunt.

And then, before he could change and fly off, he sensed something.

Him again, Langst thought. He concentrated but could not reach them. He was too far away from Kali to interfere.

He did not like this outsider knowing about them. He could not let it continue.

"I'm sure about it, Herman," Michael said after giving his mentor a brief summation of Aaron's story and problem. "She had set a compulsion in his mind, a compulsion to find her. They spoke telepathically, and she admitted her origins."

The older man's voice lost its tiredness and became excited. "Bring him to me, Michael. Quickly."

"Tomorrow," he promised.

"I'll wait at my office in the lab," Gable told him before hanging up.

Michael looked out the glass door and saw Aaron staring up at the starry sky. He sensed the tension and need radiating from Aaron and wished he could help him to relax.

Before joining Aaron outside, Michael called the airlines. He changed their reservations to an earlier flight to Dallas, arranged for a layover so that Aaron could get his computer, and confirmed their connecting flight to D.C. The operator assured him that they would arrive in Washington tomorrow night.

When that was done, Michael went out to

the patio. "Gable expects us tomorrow night. I changed our flight to an earlier one."

"I still don't know how Gable can help us," Aaron said. "People think he went around the bend twenty years ago. The only name anyone used when they talked about him was Ghostchaser."

"None of that matters. Herman Gable has his finger on the pulse of the paranormal world. What I mean by that is that if anything is happening, anywhere in this country, Herman knows about it."

"What makes you so certain?"

"Trust me, White Man. Just remember, our first step is to see him, tell him what we know, and hope that he has information that will help us."

"Unless he thinks we're crazy."

Michael shook his head. "He won't, Aaron. He's been waiting for this all his life."

"Waiting for what?" he asked.

"For Kali. For you. His research has always leaned toward parallel world theories. He believes in their existence, as I do. Aaron, with Gable's help, we can find her."

Aaron stared at his friend for several moments. "I'm not trying to find her so that she can be turned into a lab experiment for Gable."

"He wouldn't do that, Aaron."

"We don't need him."

"If I'm right, and I'm sure I am, you need him and his knowledge."

Aaron closed his eyes. "The man's senile. He's eighty."

"Eighty-four," Michael responded. "And he's far from senile. Besides, who else do we have?"

"You're crazy," Aaron stated.

"I'm crazy, am I?" Michael asked, raising a single eyebrow. "Am I the one who came to you to look for a telepath from a parallel world who brought me back from death?"

Aaron had no argument for that.

"Aaron, you haven't slept for two days. You're tired, and you're not thinking straight. Get some sleep. We're leaving at three."

"All right," Aaron whispered. "Have I thanked you yet?"

"For what?"

Aaron gazed at his friend and placed his hand on Michael's shoulder. "For believing me. For helping me."

"No."

"Thank you."

"Go to sleep, White Man."

Aaron left the patio and went into Michael's guest bedroom. He didn't bother to get undressed; he just lay on top of the cover and closed his eyes. Although he was physically tired his mind was still speeding. He thought back to the cavern, to the drawings, and to the strange electrical barrier within the cave.

Doorway, he thought. Is it possible? Am I crazy? His body tensed and his muscles trembled. Slowly, he willed himself to relax, and as he did, he thought of Kali. He pictured her as he had seen her on the golden plateau. He felt again the familiar, warm caress of her mind within his. And he knew he had to try and reach her again.

You won't need the drug anymore. You can do it by yourself, Kali had told him.

Carefully, he erased all thoughts from his mind. Slowly, he began to project and push his thoughts skyward. This time the wrenching sensation came quicker and was less violent. In an instant, he was moving through the star-strewn universe and focusing upon the infinite rainbow colors of the astral plane.

Just as suddenly, he was at the golden plateau, walking upon its soft grass. He thought of Kali and pictured her walking toward him, but when he looked for her, she was not there. Instead, he felt an alien force. He smelled the putrescent odor of that other being and, in the distance, saw a speck moving toward him. When it was closer, it looked like a man. He watched, fascinated and not a little fearful, as it grew larger. When the man got close enough to be seen, the man began to waver and then coalesce into another form. Aaron found himself staring at the glowing green eyes of a black leopard. The smell of its fetid breath was that of decaying flesh, the same scent that he had not been able to identify before.

Not real! he told himself as fear tried to hold his mind a prisoner. But he could smell and see the thing. It seemed as real as he, himself, was.

Facing the oncoming vileness that was projected at him from those evil green eyes, Aaron stood his ground and refused to be frightened away. Waves of energy hit him, thoughts so strong they were akin to a physical blow.

As the black leopard continued toward him, Aaron knew this was not happening in flesh and blood. But Aaron also knew it was real nonetheless.

His eyes locked with the panther's. He experienced the cold evil of the other's mind and shrank away.

The panther stopped moving and stared at Aaron. He fought to hold himself strong against this enemy, but he was unable to stop himself from being invaded. This being, whatever it might be, was violating his mind and thoughts. He reached within himself, searching for the power to push the intruder away.

He failed, and his mind was filled with scenes of death and torture that were so loathsome that they were almost beyond belief.

Suddenly, the cold invasion withdrew, leaving in its wake a haunting laughter that echoed in his mind. With that laughter, the fear he had been holding at bay flared.

Who are you? Aaron flung the thought at the animal with every ounce of his remaining strength.

The panther took another step forward. As

it did, Aaron's mind erupted with pain as the panther gave vent to a horrific howl that turned into a single word.

DEATH!

Then the black leopard rushed at him. When it was a dozen feet away, it left the ground. Its mouth opened to expose long glinting fangs that looked more like the gates of hell than teeth.

Battling the fear that held him immobile in the face of this oncoming death, Aaron shook himself free and instinctively withdrew from the astral plane. He catapulted his thoughts from the golden plateau and sent his mind back to his body. Through it all, the dark and evil laughter continued to vibrate within his mind.

A heartbeat later he opened his eyes and focused on the white painted ceiling of the bedroom.

His breathing was forced. His body was bathed in sweat. A chill spread across his skin. Forcing himself to breathe calmly, Aaron tried to figure out what had happened, but all he knew for certain was that someone, or something, was blocking Kali from him.

Then another disturbing thought intruded. Whoever the entity was that he'd met on the astral plane could already have Kali. Closing his eyes, Aaron willed his adrenaline-saturated body to calm down.

When his body and mind were relaxed, Aaron reasoned that if he could project himself to the astral plane, he might also be able to project his thoughts to Kali herself.

Slowly, carefully, Aaron built a picture of Kali within his mind. He thought back to the area where he had first seen her on the road outside of Sperry Hollow. Concentrating totally, Aaron launched his thoughts toward that area and to Kali.

His hands were balled into fists. The muscles in his neck knotted powerfully as he built up his thoughts of her. Then, using every ounce of energy he possessed, he sent out his thoughts of her laced with his need for her.

And then he touched her mind. He felt the gentle presence of her thoughts. *Kali.*

Go, Aaron. For your own good, get away! But even as she tried to send him away, he read the emanation of her own emotions for him.

I'm coming for you.

He will kill you. He knows you are trying to find me.

Who? The one I met on our plateau?

He was there? Langst was there?

A black leopard. Aaron sensed a new fear riding on Kali's thoughts.

Think about what happened so that I may see.

Aaron brought up the memory of the black leopard.

Langst. He was waiting for you. He blocked your thoughts from reaching me.

But not now. Why?

He plays his games. He is insane.
We are coming tomorrow.
Don't forfeit your life because of me.
We are coming for you.
Be careful, my love.

As soon as those last thoughts reached his mind, Aaron felt her presence dissolve.

"I will be careful," he promised her.

For a long time after his thoughts and Kali's had parted, Aaron's mind worked at a furious pace. Although he had wanted to believe Michael, when his friend had espoused his parallel world theory and his theory about the metaphysical beings that lived on that other world, he had not been able to really accept that.

But after encountering the black leopard, Aaron was no longer positive about anything, least of all his doubts about Michael's theory.

Finally, the lack of sleep caught up with him. Aaron's mind gave into his exhausted body's need for rest. He fell into a deep and dreamless sleep.

Don't Miss These Novels of Bone-chilling Horror from Leisure Books!